TRY NOT TO GET DISCOURAGED

Stories by John Waterfall

Cover by Zach Dodson
Book Design by Taylor A. Bingham

First Lost Fox Paperback Edition: October 2021

Paperback ISBN: 978-1-954683-02-0
Ebook ISBN: 978-1-954683-03-7

Lost Fox Publishing
hello@lostfoxpublishing.com

lostfoxpublishing.com
ig: @lostfoxpublishing
tw: @lostfoxpublish

CONTENTS

AUTHOR'S NOTE

This is a collection of derivative fiction. That's not to say I'm not proud of it. But like most writers, I learned all I know from imitating other writers, so this little collection is a bit beholden to their ghosts. As such, I'd like to thank my favorites: Cormac McCarthy, who showed me how to make language sing; Kurt Vonnegut, (who is an actual ghost) for teaching me comedic timing, and Stephen Graham Jones, for showing me that horror stories are oftentimes love stories.

ACKNOWLEDGMENTS

Bite Marks
Drunk Monkeys - 2019

Benni Goes Feral
Great Ape - 2020

The Genealogy of Pops
The Colored Lens -2019

Goodbye Blue 42
MYTHIC - June - 2020

Hector of Troy Communes with Scott Norwood in the Afterlife
Crack the Spine - 2019
Alternating Current - 2020

Levi's Song
Tales From the Deep Anthology - Flying Ketchup Press - Summer 2020

That Rambling Shambling Password Man
Cease, Cows - 2019
Unnerving Press - 2020

The Fugitive Finds Christ
Ghostlight Magazine - Fall 2020

The Sneakaboo
Pseudopod - October 2020

Shuffler (Do No Harm)
Ripples in Space Podcast - 2019
Jersey Devil Press - 2019

What Remains of the Great Alchemist
XVIII Anthology - Underland Press - Spring 2020

World's Largest Turnip
Gold Wake Live - June - 2020

Wowee-Zowee (Sudden Death)
Coffin Bell - 2019

THANK YOUS

I'd like to thank all the publishers mentioned in the acknowledgments for giving these stories homes back when they had no place else to go. Special thanks to Kolleen Carney over at Drunk Monkeys for giving me my first acceptance and for informing me of my bad grammar. Unfortunately, my grammar is still bad. Oh well. Moving on, I'd like to thank Lost Fox for giving this collection a home back when it had no place to go. And I'd like to thank my wife Tullia for giving me a home back when I had no place to go. Thank you for tolerating my mania and constant singing.

Thanks to my writing illuminati: David, Avi, Gabe, and Mike. Additional thanks to Mike for graciously proofing several of these stories, and David for being an excellent role model in this back-breaking industry. Thank you to my back, which got stronger with each rejection, I think. It still breaks occasionally.

To my father, without whom I would not be able to do this. He worked very hard in his life to provide me with privilege and opportunity. One day I hope to be able to give those things back. Hopefully, one day, privilege and opportunity will be like bowling shoes, just part of the game. Miss you pops, wish you were here.

Thanks to The New School for giving me a fantastic place to incubate. For teaching me to help other writers instead of knife fighting them to the death. My teachers: Shelley Jackson, John Reed, Patrick McGrath, Darcey Steinke, Susan Bell and Elizabeth Gaffney.

Finally, to my girl Nora. This one's for you. In the future, if I'm lucky enough to put a few more of these things together, those ones will be for you too. Even if I dedicate them to someone else, it'll be a lie. Love you kiddo. Big hug.

Some nights I try to see Jesus.
I do it by crossing my eyes.
I was doing fine then a few people died.
I was doing alright then a few people died.

- Craig Finn

GOODBYE BLUE 42

I met my wife for the first time at an art installation in Kennedy airport, terminal B. She was thirteen years old, a little black girl from Sierra Leone crowdfunding her education in a glass dome by a moving walkway. There she was, seated at a laminated desk in a yellow floral print dress, flanked on either side by two ivory white, animatronic children scribbling circles. Behind them a green-board asked the public to 'pay for the future.' Built into the front of the dome was a pin-pad and dollar feed, the transplanted face of a vending machine. For one hundred dollars you could punch in what the captive student would study, video lectures and archival footage winking into reality across the surface of the dome.

This was when I was moving around the galaxy doing investigative insurance claims work, being paid to suggest there was no fault to be had in faulty machinery. New York was on the precipice of becoming a real shithole so the airports were ghost towns. Each time we met it felt staged, like she had been propped up for my guilt or redemption. That was our courtship. It was over a decade for her. For me it was one long binge. One year of planet hopping and special relativity, coming and going through terminal B and writing up reports against policyholders that asphyxiated themselves in the badlands of Mars, of Venus, of really anywhere. It's really only badlands out there. And I'd see her, and she'd be older and smarter and knowing something she either wanted to know or didn't, such as the collected works of Marcel Proust or aliens in the bible.

That first time we met, I went to one knee and asked how she was doing, trying to play the kind stranger, not realizing my bloodshot eyes and crumpled suit made me look like someone who sold drugs from a limo. She looked like a poster child for famine relief, dressed up to stand next to the aged beneficence of Ellen DeGeneres, giving third world puppy eyes in a late-night commercial.

I asked her what she wanted to learn about. She screwed her foot into the ground and said she didn't know, her English soft, the vowels elongated. I punched a few keys and ended up in Marine Biology, specifically the care and maintenance of large sea mammals in captivity. The curved immensity of the extinct Blue Whale summoned itself onto the glass between us, tinting her with an aquatic dimness that turned her ultramarine.

"How about something with whales, honey?" I said, inserting a crumpled bill into the feed. She smiled at me through two fighting walruses; the image of her gap-toothed childhood beamed into my retinas. This is the memory I have the hardest time coming to grips with, mostly because I love it so much, and loving it makes me feel like a fiend.

***

The next time I saw her was after four months of 'me' time, fresh off a jag through the mineral planets, witnessing and notarizing the various small failures in life support equipment and the permanent, large failures in their users. At that point I'd seen pretty much every form of death you could imagine, imploded and exploded, frozen and fried.

The last incident, a cryogenic failure with a smashed face, had me thinking of quitting, but the idea of immobility seemed like death. Nobody with money tried to live in any one place anymore. Most places weren't very livable when compared to the smooth jazz purgatories of airport living. We were a generation of intransigents mulling end times, spending our lives sleeping on the tiled floors of transit hubs, waiting for the blast offs that would send us around the solar system to hawk heavy metals and life insurance.

It had been a bad flight, hours of thought directed towards the faults and responsibilities of a smashed face, the sound a flash-frozen body makes when it becomes something you can sweep up. I'd tried working on my novel, the eco-apocalypse trials of gruff Irish PI Danny Temple, and it went alright until I found out that my seatmate, a bloodshot Slavic businessman I dubbed Swiss Robinson, was working on something similar, only with an Icelandic ex-cop. We spent the rest of the flight in a small war, angling to see each other's monitors and fighting for leg space.

During arrival I spilled the remainder of my ginger ale on Swiss Robinson and watched the deterioration of New York from the window, looking for which neighborhoods had burned down, which had scaffolded back up. The city was constantly on fire, a weather system of grease and scorched stone unfolding between the hurricanes that patrolled the east coast. As the tarry city came up to meet me, I chewed three amphetamine gummies and prepared for whatever dislocation I might feel, energized to measure what was old and new, what had marched on without me. I had missed over four years.

***

In Terminal B, grinding my teeth down the infinitude of

motorized walkways, my armpits sweating out mini vodka bottles, I saw her glass bell baking in the white glow of full spectrum wattage. A health interest drink cart had sprouted from the tile next to her installment, giant, neon, carrot-shaped kiosk throwing orange and green off the polished walls and floor. I didn't recognize her at first; she was about seventeen then, eyes connected to her display through filaments of concentration that jerked her big brown irises side to side with clockwork precision, hair piled up in a tumble atop her head, thick glasses dominating the oval of her face, neck and shoulders carrying a bazaar of native beads and pan-African metallurgy. She was sitting cross-legged on her plastic classroom chair, green tank top loosely fitting over a developed chest, flannel pajama bottoms rounding out the collegiate activist ensemble. I thought she was someone else, that they'd replaced the student in captivity every so often with a contest or some other pretense for soft abduction.

Swiss Robinson, juice in hand, had his face up against the glass, drawing a dick and balls in the turmeric-ginger tinged fog he expelled. He'd just logged one thousand dollars' worth of business ethics seminars and was leering through a video of limp and firm handshakes, upset that the captive inside wasn't over the moon about learning how to make eye contact in the workplace. He started rambling on his novel, when her attention landed on me, the shriveled suit of yesteryear.

"Hey whale man!" she cried with punchy aggression, the elongated vowels of her accent lessened, replaced by adult depth and the clipping of the American sarcasm. Swiss Robinson turned, hissed something vampiric and fled towards the stale-fat waft of the food court, hands clutching the satchel bag he carried his meal ticket in.

"You're the little African girl," I managed, conscious of studying her proximity to eighteen. I never said this wasn't creepy.

Her eyebrows shot up. "Wow. Yes. In a super reductive way yes." "Sorry."

She shrugged, having scored her point. "Don't be. I WAS a little African girl."

Buzzing at the attention, I made my way to the juice cart, the bright LED friendliness of its touchscreen hijacking my endorphins, displaying an array of beautiful people dancing in bright colors, having small orgasms over liquified vegetables, "And what are you now?" I queried.

"I don't know. Whatever happens when globalization fucks philanthropy." "Airport baby," I mused, hoping to sound every bit the silver fox I wished I was. A medium blue-moss freeze piddled into a to-go cup and ejected itself towards me, strangely warm.

The carrot thanked me.

"Sounds right enough," she murmured, picking at a toenail, glasses catching the orange glow of the great carrot, robotic, destroying in an instant my memory of the little girl in yellow with a sinister radiation. The first claws of time-loss panic gurgled in my stomach and my vision saturated yellow.

"Hey, listen," she continued, "Can you spring for some introductory Portuguese lessons? There's this hunk that cleans the bathrooms, but no ingles. I've missed out on the Latin languages entirely."

"No more whales?"

"I can't get an orgasm from a whale," my first sip of blue-moss came back up, "Also they're extinct. Except for a suicidal Beluga in Atlanta named Blue-42 and he's a ticking clock. They force feed him morning and night."

The combination of panic and whatever was in blue-moss

freeze had convinced my bowels that action was imminent. Sweat beaded at my temples, the revolt in my innards torpedoing my brief confidence at impressing this captive underage girl.

"So, they let you out of this thing?" I stammered.

"Is that a real question?" She stopped working at her nail, fixing me with something between pity and annoyance.

"I guess?"

"Where do I pee? Where do I sleep?" She motioned to her surroundings, the two mechanical children at either side had long started losing their bleached skin and had been defaced with permanent marker mustaches and devil horns. The installation had been updated to reflect the inhabitant's punkish developments, the slice of classroom emanating the appearance of an underfunded after-school prison yard. The word detention was scribbled in chalk across the green board and one of the dummies' fingers had found its way into a mechanical nostril.

"I hadn't thought of that."

"Inside every white dude there's a captivity fantasy. It's the product of a negative imagination," she mused, twirling a finger.

"Rapunzel, Rapunzel." I stabbed in my pocket for something to turn into Portuguese.

"What does that mean?"

"Nothing. It means nothing." I stuffed a tired bill into the interface, the archaic vending machine-mouth rejecting it with a gag until it didn't.

"I live in the Sheraton with two other girls. North Korean poor and rust belt poor. We rotate."

"You take turns being poor?" Even in my growing sickness I

couldn't help conjuring an international pillow fight.

"Being the student," she sighed.

"Well, take it easy," I stammered amid a retreat to the bathroom. I took a final look at her as I went, a girl on the cusp of a strange adulthood, raised on technology and passing interests.

"They named him after a football thing," she called after me. "What?"

"The whale. Blue-42. It's something a quarterback says. Blue-42! Hut! Hut!"

Her words chased me as I moved, trying to run and keep my butt cheeks clenched at the same time. I have no idea why she married me.

***

I spent the night in the city, rejuvenated by the recent evacuation of trans-galaxy mid-flight cuisine and airport smoothies. Outside a storm was in mid explosion, the churning sky veined with lightning, gale force winds slapping the low slung, heavy vehicles built to withstand their force, movable bunkers. My cab took the Ellen DeGeneres memorial expressway to the FDR bridge, the lights of the great Atlantic Seawall, a necklace of red dots looped around the circumference of the horizon. Manhattan spilled itself in front of me, an oil slick of light and water, the twinkling infinitude of skyscraper lights and bodega neon doubled in the brackish moats and canals. We took the elevated superhighway to the newly renovated Port Authority, proud home to Carnival Cruises. I waited for the storm to die with the cackling bums, till 3 A.M, when the angry weather turned into an eerie stillness irradiated with leftover ozone.

A water taxi took me to my mom's place, the building

I grew up in. The boatman, an ancient grey-beard who pleadingly introduced himself as Kim Stanley Robinson, hummed Bruce Springsteen's *Darkness on the Edge of Town* with hymnal reverence, the shimmering corridors of the aquatic avenues around us stirred by fingers of wind that left delicate grooves in the quicksilver water. He told me he'd predicted all of this, kind of, in a best-selling novel written in 2017. He asked if I could believe that. I said that I could and when I didn't follow up, he started babbling about communes. When that didn't take, he asked me if I thought it was possible that he was a ghost.

We cruised around the edge of the park, the dead branches of the saline-choked oaks and maples reaching through the boggy surface like arthritic hands, a home to the veritable thousands of manatees that had moved in since the city went to the sea. Eventually the palace of my youth trundled into view, a giant stone fortress crowned with three oxidized brass towers, its sandy exterior gangrenous with hungry growths of sea scum crawling up its flanks, clouds of mosquitos and other bloodsuckers pixelating the searchlights that defended the lobby canopy from darkness. Kim Stanley Robinson dropped me off and took a look.

"Would've made a nice commune," he said.

***

The building had been turned into a capsule hotel; the spacious luxury apartments rendered into bite size cells of 20th century New York glamour. Only the towers remained in their entirety, penthouse homes to two former presidents and one Russian oligarch-in-exile who spent his twilight madness shooting at the Central Park manatees from an open window. I was given a room on the thirteenth floor, ending up in two-hundred square feet of my former living room, encroached upon by an island kitchenette and one-eighth of a chandelier. The gleaming wood floor remained unchanged from the days of my childhood. A section of wood grain that swirled into a pig's snout marked my familiarity. It had been a distant seventy-eight years for this place, a confusing twelve for me. My mom had been alive the last time I'd been here, the day I announced my intentions to set upon the adventure of cosmic insurance investigation with all the fervor and gusto of joining a rebellion. She died sometime between my first transit between Pluto and the Kuiper Belt, washed away with the rest of the Hamptons when hurricane season stopped ending.

I dozed on the floor, staring at the pig's snout in the wood grain, convinced that my life could expand nor reduce further, having somehow achieved an impossible equilibrium without my knowledge or permission. The tortured Beluga, Blue-42, swam through my half-conscious thoughts, fantasy nightmares of how one would force feed a Beluga. I saw its pudgy, embryonic body strapped to a laboratory gurney while aquarium tourists formed an infinity queue to force feed it books. I was in the line, balling up the pages of my finished novel into a digestible mass. When it was my turn the Beluga regarded me with shiny eyes, black orbs lubed with tears lodged into a curious white ridge. And then I started shoving.

***

I snuck by her on my way to Titan the next night, riding the moving walkway to avoid any verbal interaction. Kennedy was deserted aside from a small fleet of janitors and the occasional lump of a sleeping traveler, passed out on the floor, unable to reach a lounge before giving out.

A Japanese businessman was in the process of breaking down in front of her, sliding against her dome to his knees and wailing. She tapped the glass that separated his head from

her, petted him through her forcefield as he spat out words
I couldn't understand and paid her to learn introductory
Japanese. This teenager who would become my wife
existed entirely for me in these moments of cinema, mental
impressions, collected and filled by the things I thought she was,
implicitly.

***

My time on Titan gave me on eye twitch, some
psychosomatic response to the bobbing corpse of a gasoline
farmer who died in a way nobody scientifically understood after
a faulty railing deposited him into a lake of methane. I ruled,
'No Fault.' On my way home, a word that had started giving
me panic attacks, I bought myself a postcard of a cat riding a
dog and scribbled, "It has not been a very good day. No fault
of mine!" on the back. I no longer had a permanent residence,
so I addressed the post card to the Atlanta Aquarium, special
attention Blue-42, and put it to the mercy of the intergalactic
postal service.

Time bled from my body on the flight back in, the reality
of my situation and future written across the somber faces of
the families that traveled together to stay together, to not be
carried away apart on the temporal eddies. The idea that I had
never loved anything as much as myself crossed my mind. A
thought I quickly pushed away knowing that I had never loved
myself that much to begin with.

Then it was Terminal B again. Only this time with my
twitching eye and growing sense of self-debasement and
memory of a floating corpse. The Japanese businessman
had turned my future wife's learning experiment into a pan-
religious shrine, thronged by a gaggle of acolytes dressed
in Sheraton bathrobes and spa sandals, all kneeling within
concentric circles of burning incense bought from the duty-

free sprawl. An idyllic green landscape speckled with songbirds flitted over the glass, obscuring the woman inside into a dark shape. When I attempted to approach, the gowned loons closed ranks and asked me if I was there for the traveling business-man recovery session. I said I was not. The Japanese man emerged from the crowd, cheeks wet and peeling, as if his fit of weepiness had lasted the entire Earth year I had been away.

"You don't have to go back out there," he chanted, encouraging the crowd to join, "You don't have to go back."

From deep within the impenetrable dome, I saw her dark shape wave at me.

"What's going on?" I cried out, louder than I wanted, waving back with two jazz-fingered hands. The outline of her shrugged and the chanting grew. I ran when the hugging started.

***

That night was a layover. I tried sleeping at a Sbarro's pizza but found myself unable to drift away, my mind colonized by an imagined scenario in which Blue-42's right to suicide had gone all the way to the Supreme Court. I gave up on sleep, stole a bathrobe from the Aer Lingus lounge and creeped back to terminal B through the emptied concourse. The flock of traveling businessmen where dozing in an un-athletic pile, their voluminous bathrobes sprawled amongst the burning fragrances. The bubble lit the wide corridor with the scrolling topography of the night sky, a half-globe bright with the nodes of constellations pulsing and connecting with filaments of silver glow, the canned voice of Neil deGrasse Tyson purring out cosmic platitudes into the recycled air.

I belly-crawled through the businessmen and knocked on the dome. Her dark shape came to meet me, sliding into a matching prone position. Her hair was down, giving her silhouette a crazed, thunderstruck quality.

"Hey," I whispered, "It's me!"

"Hay is for horses," she whispered back, "Also, why are we whispering." A nearby fart froze me in terror.

"Take this seriously!" I hissed, ready for the clawed hand of a businessman to tear at my disguise, "These people are nuts."

"A little off yes, but in a harmless way. The incense does seem like a fire hazard though. How've you been?" she offered, her smoky voice dislodging something nostalgic in my chest.

"I saw a guy who somehow boiled and froze at the same time," I muttered, the image of mottled pink and blue flesh flashing across my mind.

"Gross."

"How about you?" I asked.

"I've been mostly learning about Shinto and Viva Negativa on a loop. Mr. Iwata is trying to create a sort of ashram for space-travelers. I think I'm an oracle of something."

"And how's that working out?"

She shrugged. "It's a thing that happens to me.

A stirring bathrobe caught my attention, and I froze as the owner staggered to the nearby men's room, leading my eye to the glass wall that revealed the airfield and distant city lights. I could see our reflection in the glass, a pile of worshippers huddled around a giant nightlight.

"You want to know something weird? I remember you as a child. Can you remember that about yourself? Being a child? A totally different you? You were much more African then."

"Can you see my eyes?"

"No."

"I'm rolling my eyes."

"I don't know, it just seems profound. To me."

"Well, every time I see you, you're wearing the same suit and jacket. Is that profound?" The shape of her paused, as if the observation brokered some unrealized depth.

"What's your name?" I asked.

"Naima," her shape answered. She didn't ask mine and I didn't offer it. My name has never been important. I curled up against the dome and watched its projection of the firmament, the pieces of Gemini softly tinkling across Naima's shadow, pleased to have pursued a pleasant conversation to its termination.

"I'm going to go to sleep now Airport Man," She whispered, and then she was gone, back into her curve of firmament, a spirit receded into its element.

***

A group of poisoned miners on an Alpha Centauri comet marked the end of my career in insurance. I'm not sure what happened. I'm really not. But I believe the cumulative negative stresses of dead miners and smashed faces triggered a nervous episode in which I stamped 'fault' all over my report, even though the deceased were clearly incorrect in installing their rebreathers backwards. The way I rationalize it, a human mind can only internalize the extent of the world's scariness to a point, after which it breaks. I had reached my threshold long before I'd realized it, probably on the floor of my childhood home after it had reached its own form of psychosis.

As a form of severance, I was transported to a psychiatric facility on the oceanic moon of Europa called the Deep Empathy for Persona Trauma Healing clinic, refreshingly anagrammed as D.E.P.T.H, where I was held under my own recognizance as all my relatives had died in hurricanes. I do not recall all my time at D.E.P.T.H due to the constant stream of Haldol, although I can recall the sterile, regenerative landscape of white pressure ridges and deep blue that unfurled from my window, the great banded orb of Jupiter observing my recovery.

They released me when I stopped hunger striking and trying to escape with Blue-42, who I occasionally hallucinated slumped in the bleach white visitation room, pondering the impossibility of a game of solitaire. We quickly became accomplices, my imaginary Beluga and me, secreting away utensils to dig through the walls, drawing up hypothetical floor plans, biting the nurses' fingers when they checked to see if we swallowed out medication.

We got out once. After knocking out an orderly with a metal chair we escaped to the frozen sprawl of mile deep ice that sealed away the ocean of that strange arctic world. The plan was to dig until we reached liquid, to dive and hide amongst the volcanic vents near the moon's core till our pursuers gave up the search. I was nearly dead when they found me, for a while I was very upset that they had.

At the end of my time at D.E.P.T.H. I received a reply to my wayward postcard, a glossy print of Blue-42 staring into the camera, pudgy face screwed up into what a human would call a smile. His name was signed in illegible cursive at the bottom. I also got a coupon for half-off admission to the Atlanta Aquarium. I'm not crazy anymore, but I have to say, being crazy has its perks.

***

Five years later I returned to terminal B. It had been sixth months for me. Fate or comedy had once again conspired to seat me next to Swiss Robinson on the flight into Kennedy. The smoldering remains of Simon and Schuster had just given him a seven-figure book deal, part of which he had promptly turned into a blue-velvet tuxedo and a side swipe haircut. He was magnanimous for the most part, offering me industry tips and writerly advice when he wasn't being patronizing. I trapped him in a lavatory with a drink cart after we taxied to the gate.

***

I let the tidal draw of the moving walkway pull me towards her, tumbling over the railing to the ground when I wanted to get off. The bubble was broken, clear and cracked, the vintage vending machine dollar slot smashed off its axis, mangled android students turned to face the green board with hands permanently raised. A lopsided desk and old swivel chair had found their way inside and she was seated there, twenty-four, a silk blouse and black skirt completing the image of professorial serenity. Her hair was still massive, woven into thick braids that toppled to the small of her back.

I crawled towards my future wife, hoping that I wouldn't have to fight a despondent Japanese man for her attention. I didn't have to, a certain Mr. Iwata had died in an incense related fire within the calendar year, his demise memorialized by a dark smudge on the tile that refused to be scrubbed away. He left a modest fortune to the girl he'd come to love as a divine emissary, providing her the freedom to live a life anywhere in the galaxy, an opportunity Naima was reluctant to take for reasons she would never articulate, which I intuited to be fear.

She studied me over the top of a dog-eared copy of *The Left Hand of Darkness*.

"Airport Man," she said, licking her forefinger to turn a page. "That's reductive," I said, prompting a snort of laughter from her.

"You've got a good memory. I thought those solar winds baked that away."

"Only my testicles," I conceded.

"Mmm-hmm," she sighed, lowering us into a moment of easy silence. Which I broke. "Can I come in there?" I asked.

She lowered her book and watched me, our first time in a long time, or maybe ever, of full mutual eye contact, her irises were hazel. "Are you going to attack me?" "I don't think so."

A panic button under her desk unlocked a waist high glass panel that slid upwards with a pneumatic hiss. I ducked into the classroom and deposited one of the dummies to the floor with a clatter, claiming its seat as my own.

She turned her pages in silence, once every forty seconds or so.

"What happened to the Beluga?" I asked, something vital bobbing in my throat. "Hold on I'm getting to the good part," she murmured.

"There is no good part. They get snuck in the snow and don't have sex," I replied. She stuck her tongue out at me over the top of the book and went back to reading.

"He died of acute depression," she thew out casually a page later, "About eight years ago."

"Goodbye Blue-42," I said, trying to recall my exact position in the universe when my chosen spirit animal swam off his mortal coil.

As she read, I watched the outside word, the rolling blackouts of the city's dark spread, bright penumbras of conflagrations producing soft glows on the shoulders of buildings, a scattering of sunrises.

"You know something weird?" I said, "I remember you as a child. I remember when you where this big." I raised my arm to measure out her younger self.

"Yeah, you told me that." She said,

"Well," I said, "let me tell you again."

***

It was mostly a matter of persistence. Of sitting at her bubble every day and being friends.

Of waiting out her year-and-a-half, on and off relationship with that Brazilian janitor. Of relearning what a year felt like. She taught classes from her bubble, charging whatever someone wanted to give, and I was there every day till I had given everything I owned. Even when we did get together it took us a long time to catch up, for the distance not to matter. But eventually we loved each other enough to regret what we missed in those years, which is okay, because you're going to regret something. I'm happy, and I think she is too, although I will always doubt her happiness more than my own.

We moved out to the badlands of Utah, an underground moisture farm in the expanse of a salt flat where, at night, the ground reflects the stars in a perfect mirror. Sometimes I slip out of bed and wander this strange mirage, this impressive doubling of the visible universe where I count the constellations, I learned so long ago. Sometimes she does too, and I know nothing of what spurs her twilight walkabouts.

We split time on Europa, spending more and more of our lives there with each trip. I don't work on my novel anymore, whatever observations I had about the ending of things seems exhausted. Instead, I've shifted my focus to a chronicling of the extinct Beluga whale, the canary of the sea, the only cetacean to ever have a neck. And sometimes I listen to the sounds in Europa's one great ocean, underneath the ice, to see if I can hear anything that sounds familiar.

I'm sometimes hit over the head with the fact that I met my wife when she was a child and I was a man. It got less weird, because she grew up, but I still have that memory of seeing her for the first time, because how could I forget. Yet it still jumps into my brain when we're intimate, when I imagine the daughter we're not able to have, because the starlight cooked my soldiers. I don't like that. She says not to worry. She says thoughts have many faces. But still, I wonder and worry, because after I saw her, that first time, in my head I said, *who wouldn't want to have a kid like that.*

BITE MARKS

He was laying on the grass when she came back, staring at the leaves overhead rustling loose from their branches, sunlight dripping through. It was windy and suddenly she was there, summoned between blinks, her head and hair a dark silhouette.

"I'm back," she said, walking past him through the front door and into the house, leaving him to the crisp autumn, the sweep of yellow and orange that erupted from the front lawn, the hedge that hid the bumpy road to the sea. He watched the leaves, the parched dry shapes clinging, heart pounding a rhythm in his chest. Then he got up and went after her, in an effort to check his head.

She was in the kitchen, going through the fridge, popping beer cans and tasting a sip from each, seven cans lined up already on the white linoleum countertop. She was in jeans and a metal t-shirt he'd remembered her wearing, band name splatted in a red arc around a mad dragon eating an exploding missile.

"I fucking hate beer," she complained, wincing in response to a sip of Pork Slap. He found himself speaking without thinking, "Well, if I'd known you were coming."

She snorted a laugh, beer foaming from her nose. "Shit. Oh, that's funny. You're handling this well."

He looked at her, the same pale oval of a face, honey blonde hair, thick and catching the stray light behind it in a halo, individual strands wigged out like lightning bolts. Beautiful hair. He liked to smell it with his face in the hollow of her neck, feeling her pulse in his eyes.

"I'm very confused," he managed to stammer. "I'm making my rounds."

"You're dead."

"Sure am."

He pulled out a wooden high-stool and sat at the linoleum island, watching her unbelievable shape. She was how he'd last seen her, the size and shape and color she was when she'd descended the subway escalator in Cambridge, leaving him alone on the surface where it had ended.

He squinted and rubbed his eyes. "This is insane. This isn't a real thing." The sunlight in the room intensified, a liquid gold that slanted through the windows as the day marched towards dusk.

"Yeah well, I don't love it either." She shrugged and leaned on her elbows opposite him. He hadn't remembered her face, had been approximating it in a memory blur, the tan skin, pale lips, a sternness that fought the relaxed way her hair fell, the softness in her face, beautiful in a way you realized later, the round politician's jaw.

"You've been gone for seven years."

"Seven years, eight months, twelve days, four hours, and six minutes. Seven now."

"Holly shit."

"Look if you can't deal with this we're going to have a bad time." "Are you haunting me? Did I do something?"

"I'm hooking up with you," she said while investigating a nail, like it was a fact, the next day's weather. He felt his blood rush downwards, making him hard. He'd thought about this for years, sleeping with her again, fucking her in a power sort of way. This was before she'd died horribly, after which he'd thought about it much less until not at all. It hadn't hit him until then, that she'd had a story he wasn't a part of. Then he was horrified, that what happened could happen, that it happened to her.

"Why?"

"Because I'm here. You don't want to?"

"I'm married." She seemed hurt, which made him feel good, for a moment, then bad because whatever was happening was too much, that his obsession with her hadn't died but only been dormant and waiting to manifest.

"That's nice. Is she nice?"

"She's nice." He thought of his wife, the curl of their child in her belly, the puzzle fit of their sleeping bodies. And he saw that the girl in front of him was sad and bored, that she was turning a soft translucent.

"Good," The ghost of her whispered, "It's good to be nice."

He thought about saying her name, then she was gone. He stood in near silence, the soft wind and the occasional chirp of birds playing across the amber light. The beers were still there, seven cans of different colored chromes, sparkling in the waning day. And he stood there till all the colors looked the same in the dark.

***

He found himself outside, under the tree, searching the grass for a body he could return to, in case he'd lost his mind or died himself. There was his divot, the man shaped impression in the grass, forest green in the neon blue dark, first stars twinkling bright and white, a full moon heavy and pearlescent. The urge to leave flickered across his mind, to get into his car and drive, to flee the ghost who'd boomeranged back.

He made it as far as the driveway, the car idling at the lip of the outside world. Through the rearview mirror he saw a dark bulk shuffle across the driveway and around the garage, disappearing into the milky night with a loud, breathy snort. His balls crawled into his gut. He turned the car around and searched the surrounding darkness with the high-beams, wiggling the front of the vehicle left and right to get a glimpse at whatever strangeness had gone lumbering by. Satisfied he parked and got out, foot landing in a round depression, a large paw print in the gravel that filled and erased itself as he watched, leaving only the long finger marks of claws. A loamy breeze brought salt and earth to his tongue and a sea fog rolled in from the murmuring ocean, the driveway and road coming alive in the smell and sound. Somewhere in the dark something breathed, heavy and wet and he could hear the crunch of gravel as it moved. He knew he would stay.

***

An hour later she was waiting outside the shower, a fogged outline of jeans and black tee. He drew a circle in the moisture and cleared it. She was eating an apple. He got out and watched her eat the sticker.

She shrugged and picked it out of her teeth, balled it and flicked it. "You're fat now." "It's been eleven years," he retorted, trying to hide the hit nerve.

She turned towards the mirror, a dull silver square over a

single porcelain sink, the place where his parents used to brush their teeth, a catalogue of gap mouthed fish and the lures to catch them leaping from the surrounding wallpaper: mayfly for trout, nightcrawler for pike. The night outside was dark against the room's burst of fluorescent yellow, the window a square of hard black.

"What do I look like?" she asked, studying the mirror. He saw only himself in the reflection, paunch spilling over the towel wrapped around his waist. He wasn't ashamed, wasn't embarrassed. If she was real, she'd seen it before. If she wasn't, he was having bigger problems.

"Twenty. The last time I saw you. Wearing the Clutch shirt you got from the Paradise Rock show."

"Clutch sucks."

"It was your shirt," he said, shifting the towel to his head and face, flabby adulthood on full display, his voice muffled through the soft fabric, "So what? You crossed Styx to call me fat?"

"I told you. I came here to sleep with you." "Why?"

"What else do you want to do?"

"We could talk?"

"What do you want to talk about? Because I really don't want to talk. It's been eleven years. And I know we're going to, but I want to do this first. It'll help the talking."

"I'm married," he protested, his body making a decision for itself. He readjusted the towel and took a gulp of wet air. If she'd noticed she hadn't said anything, she was elsewhere, eyes slit in hard thought. The mirror had fogged and he could no longer see himself.

"I was going to be. Venue and everything. Then a bear ate me."

"I heard." He saw a small rigidness build in her, a break in her practiced languidness. "Look," she said, "you made your decision in the driveway. This isn't real, not in the same way. And you know what would be nice for me? An orgasm. Because believe it or not, for me, this isn't about you. When I get see my fiancé, whenever I get to pop into existence around him, then I want to fucking talk, but right now, probably for the only time, I'm stuck with you, so can we just do it already?

He thought about the guilt ghost sex would have on his relationship, but not very hard. "Yeah sure, okay."

***

Her body rolled on top of his in the pale light of his old room, the place of his first time with her, this strange new time. Blue light poured in from the windows on the outer walls, catching her body in pools and shadows. He felt her warmth, the softness of her hips and breasts as he reluctantly cupped her, then less reluctantly as he felt the warmth between them spread, the extension of selves between. She didn't look at him, eyes focused behind shut lids, reaching for release or thoughts of someone else, her hair tangled and matted with sweat, the honey, earthen scent of her filling his senses. He pulled her down to him, equaling her physically, one hand in her hair, the other kneading her backside. And then she went and so did he, and in the moment, she flickered, in and out of reality. In strobes he could see his release in the air, free in a blink than caught and contained within her body. He closed his eyes and felt her go into thin air, and a single damp pearl landed on the bed beside him.

When he couldn't sleep, he went to the window to watch the moon bright world, the dark hints of deer grazing in the lawn. Amidst the herd stood a large shape on hind legs, a fuzzy hulk bobbing its tapered snout to the heavens, sniffing at the air for a scent on the breeze.

***

When he woke up to dawn-light she was nestled in the crook of his arm and he was breathing her scent, the warm air that escaped her mouth rhythmically lapping the skin of his forearm. He watched the hairs moving with each breath, and everything was silent besides their soft rustle, the occasional nightingale call out in the glowing world.

"Is it like this for everyone?" he asked.

"I don't know. I'm not everyone." She shifted and he realized his arm was asleep, tingling dully under her weight. He started to pull it out from under her and he saw the movement made her dissolve in places, gashes of ragged white static spreading across her thigh and shoulder, her neck, the bite marks where she'd been unmade. He resumed his grasp, hoping to undo the damage.

"Did it hurt?"

"It wasn't as bad as it sounded. All the gruesome stuff happened after I was dead." He found the lobe of her ear, the lock of hair that circled it, ingrained tokens of his intimacy that now belonged elsewhere. "The worst part was other people's memory of it, people knowing that it happened to me. The infamy. The bad part's infamy. No one will ever think of my story without thinking of the end."

He'd thought about it, imagined it, everything from the look on her face before and during, the horror movie scream, the strewn aftermath of a hungry brown shape ravaging a Yosemite campsite. Outside the bedroom he could hear something large, sniffing and shuffling, hot bestial grunts excavating the crack under the door, floorboards creaking in retaliation to a massive weight.

"What's that?" he asked, surprised by the lack of alarm in his half-sleep drawl. For a moment he saw himself getting up and opening the door to the creature pawing outside, two eyes of animal black hovering over a primordial snout, a white grimace of teeth.

"Ignore it." "Can it get-"

"Ignore it." She sighed. He felt comforted by her weariness. Whatever this was, it wasn't a nightmare for him, which was as far as he could see. The seconds accrued between them and he thought she'd fallen back asleep.

Falling into his own dream he heard her, "My dad saw me as a four-year-old, dressed up like a tea-cup for Halloween. Nearly lost his mind when I drank all his gin." He felt the muscles in her face tighten and smile, felt his own.

"That's funny." "Yeah, it's funny."

***

They slept-in together, dozing in the body warmed sheets, the morning outside grey and raining. They were silent and physical, communicating through touches and squeezes, each focused on what was next, when it would be over. The thing that had been done, done again.

When the rain cleared, they walked down the road to the sea, the babbling surf murmuring to them as they made their way over granite, wisps of fog curling around their feet, the air in the middle distance brushed with undulating webs of cloud. He held her hand when they were alone, dropped it when someone drove by so he wouldn't look crazy.

They sat together at the surf and waited for it to happen,

watching the frothy lead-colored waves push in and out, crawling over the packed sand to clutch at their ankles. She buried her feet, biting her lip in concentration as she evaluated the feeling of sand between her toes.

"Look," she said, "I want you to know I loved you. You were one of the people I loved.

"You were a nice piece of my life."

He nodded, searching for something deep to say, "Who do you go to next?"

"I don't know. I hope my dad. My fiancé, he's living in an ashram now, gonna see if I can break him out of it. The time I'm gone gets longer each go-around."

"What's that like?"

"It's not like anything. I'm just gone." She looked at him, studied his face and he saw her back full, locked in pleasantly uncomfortable eye contact. She had yellow in the blue of her irises, she had a freckle beneath the curve of a nostril. "This might be it for you. I don't know if I'll come back this way."

"Yeah. You're probably right," he added, looking at the speck of a person on the beach horizon, a small dark spot throwing a tennis ball to another, smaller spot. "Here's what I'll do. Every time I see someone faraway, I'll tell myself it's you. What do you think?"

But she didn't think anything because she wasn't there and he was talking to himself, the depression in the sand where she'd been slowly erasing in the salty breeze. He sat there and felt practiced, like he'd over-reached and said something scripted, which was how she'd always made him feel.

A great shape emerged from behind him and entered his peripheral. A bear, shaggy and dour, thick brown coat tangled and knotted in the damp sea air. It sniffed at the air pensively, pawed the sand and looked at him, grey light twinkling in obsidian eyes. It gathered itself with a snort and trudged towards the sea, disappearing into the curled palm of a coming wave, the scent of hide vanquished in salt spray. He sat and wondered how long it would take for it to all feel like a dream.

BENNI GOES FERAL

There is no sound like the sound of the Mourning Dove. It reminds me of the time my sister died. It was at the beginning of the cold season, and I was asleep in the comfy chair, and I heard its *hooing* in and out, in and out. There was a cold dry air with the light going away, and on it I could smell dead leaves, and outside I could see the individual blades of grass stir and move and the many, many dead bats that covered the lawn. Then I stretched and meowed, and I walked by the corpse of my giant, who had exploded his mouth and head and died because he was very sad.

I padded to the porch door which never closed anymore because I had moved a shoe there to block it. There I looked out into the deepening blue, into a sky that was bleeding its color away at the cloudy fringes. Giant had loved these late skies because of 'red.' I do not know exactly what 'red' is, other than it is a color I cannot see. My sister was this color, was this 'red,' although she looked grey to me. This makes me sad because if I could see 'red' then maybe I wouldn't forget her. I forget things now. I think I am forgetting how to be a cat. Giant was the cat expert despite not being one. He knew all things I should and should not do to be a good cat, taught me special things like words and not to go on the countertop because it is a place of sacred energy.

Sometimes I like to think that it wasn't her that died, that it was some other 'red' cat that got scooped up by an owl, that maybe she just wandered off, that maybe she finally found the courage to be wild again. And this makes me both happy and sad. Because I know it isn't true. I know she is dead. Because I saw it.

On the porch I called to her, rumbling a noise from a humming place in my throat, a sound I had made just for her. I could see the little waves the noise made as it went out to search, disturbing the ready to sleep air. I stretched. The Mourning Dove's call disappeared into the cricket buzz of the bright dark, and it was quiet because the world was afraid. My spine crept and I went flat because I was also afraid, and from the yard came the deep stuttering call of an owl, a dark question, echoing from the great pine tree that stood apart from the wall of the forest, like the other trees were afraid of it. I saw it there among the branches, a great horned darkness with her shape slack in its talons, saying nothing, the descending sun heavy and large behind it. And it called again, summoning a wind that toyed with the wings of the dead bats on the lawn like it was pulling them back to life. Her name was Apricots, and she was not good at being a cat. She would bite Giant and hiss things like, "Apricots is my slave name!" She died when an owl plucked her from the world. It could have eaten all the dead bats it wanted to, but it took her just the same. And then I was all alone.

***

My name is Benni and I am trying to remember things. Each day spent alone makes me less good at being a cat, makes it harder to do the things cats do like use the litter box and not drink from the toilet. All the things Giant taught me.

My interest in killing has gone way up since Giant and Apricots died. Which is sad and exciting. I do not want to lose my higher functions, the contemplative mystery of the ceiling fan, how Apricots' flank smell-touched against mine, the earthy taste of her fur. I have exciting, arousing dreams where I groom her and my tic-tac comes out, but mostly I dream about dead mice and dead mice heads and dead mice babies.

I'm scratching the contents of my head into the walls and furniture of the forest house, for anyone who wants to read it, or for myself, in case I return to my history as a stranger, and I won't ever be alone because I'll have these stories. I've started my notes on the comfy chair, which previously was a big no-no because it belonged to Giant and led to sprays from the spray bottle. I'm beginning to think that perhaps Giant did not know as much about being a cat as he let on. For example, yesterday I chased a moth to the sacred countertop where I killed and ate it, smashing it a little for fun, and nothing happened! Everything was totally fine! And I got a really good look at the kitchen and knocked the horrible spray bottle to the floor where it can never spray again. Maybe Giant was selfish and wanted all these fun things to himself. But even with all these fun things, Giant didn't want to be alive anymore after his children died from 'flu.' Most of the giants died from 'flu.'

I cannot see 'flu,' like I cannot see 'red.' If I could, I would have tried to bite it and eat its head before it killed Giant's small giants. Maybe 'flu' is still here? Waiting in the under-couch spaces. Coming up with plans to make my life worse. Maybe 'flu' is making me less good at being a cat.

I'm not sure the children were meant to be with us. In the days before we left for the forest house Giant screamed things into the air like, "I can make them safe!" and, "Goddamit! They're my kids too Jeanine!" The children always made Giant sad, even when they came over and slept on the floor Giant

would act happy while moving sad. And when they left he
would cry and cry.

***

Apricots was not a big fan of being a cat. She had lived in
the parking lot of a library before Giant brought her home to
be my sister, or as she put it, abducted her. The library parking
lot was tough living, bad giants occasionally did things like
skateboard over her paws and tie firecrackers to her tail, all of
which turned Apricots slightly crazy. I did my best with her,
showed her who was big cat and who was little cat. But she
always got back up, never submitted to what I had to show her
about living indoors.

Apricots believed that the truest way to be a cat was to do
the opposite of what any cat expert demanded: that good cats
were outside cats, not inside cats, which, as per Giant's wisdom,
was heresy. This was why she sometimes peed on Giant's
lap and bit his ankles. Or so she said. I don't know that many
words, but I do know about something called "compensating,"
which was the reason Giant fed his children pizza and ice cream
whenever they stayed with us. Apricots was tough to be sure,
but she ate from the food bowl like I did, slept by the fire like
I did, and accepted the belly rubs just like I did. And she was
beautiful and strange and a very, very bad cat.

She had no fur on one knee and half a right ear. If there is
one good thing about my deteriorating condition it is that I am
becoming the wild cat she always wished I was.

***

The porch door is shut because a raccoon stole the shoe
and decided to move in. Now I am trapped inside with the
shoe-stealing raccoon and cannot reach my supply of dead bats.

The raccoon lives inside the sofa and squawks at me when I try to write my stories. It is big and dark and scary like a bush with teeth. Perhaps I can find a way to kill it. Perhaps I can trap it in the toilet while it drinks up all my water. I imagine intelligence is on my side as the raccoon chose a shoe over freedom, trapping us both here, but then again, now, starvation is against us both.

There's just me and it, and Giant's smelly body. Every now and then I lose consciousness only to wake up in the middle of gnawing one of Giant's fingers. I think I may have eaten the wedding ring he refused to take off, as my stomach feels like a pinecone. This is not good cat behavior.

***

I tried to mate with Apricots several times, despite having no balls. She would be sleeping or dozing on the comfy chair, which was really mine when Giant wasn't looking, and I'd jump up to bite her a little and remind her how mine it was only to end up on top of her and curling my lower body towards her butt. She was a good sport about it, letting me try to do this thing I had only half knowledge of before twisting around and biting my nose. I believe if I had balls, things would have been different, that we would have been mates and not siblings, even if I was, as she described, "a little cat in a big cat body." She really was wonderful, in a real-life sort of way. Sometimes things that sound mean can actually be very nice, like nose biting. Now that she's gone I try mating with a foam football. Perhaps that is something that does not need to be recorded.

***

The toilet trap worked wonderfully until it did not. I managed to shut the lid on top of the greedy interloper but

keeping a desperate raccoon trapped inside of a toilet is not
an easy thing to do. It's a scary thing to do, because of the
squawking and the clawed hands that reach out with every
bump of the lid, searching around for something to punish.
I think there is something deeply wrong with the Raccoon.
Perhaps 'flu.' It foams from the mouth and cannot control its
swiveling golden eyes, bounding headlong into the walls till
it falls into convulsive sleep. I am reminded of Giant. Giant
used to bang his head against things as well. Sometimes, late at
night, Giant would pack us up in the car along with a knapsack
filled with snacks and wait outside a house in the darkness.
Sometimes his children would come and go with the woman
Jeanine and Giant would lie down in his seat and hold his
breath. Apricots and I did not like these trips and I would start
to freak out a little, sensing something bad about to happen.
And Apricots would tell me to shut up and Giant would tell us
both to shut up and then start to bang his head on the wheel.
I think I am starting to paint Giant in a bad light. Being his
cat wasn't always sad and uncomfortable. Sometimes Giant
would bury his face in my side and cry and cry. Which was
uncomfortable but also nice.

***

I find that scratching my story is simply reliving my story.
The only story I remember well enough now is the story in
which Apricots dies. Which disappoints me because the only
thing I get to relive is Apricots dying. Which was not the point
of this exercise, which was to remain a cat and remember loved
ones and good times. The problem is I do not fully understand
what I have scratched, or I forget what my marks and smells
meant at the time that I made them. So, I cannot read the
memory perfectly. The more I try not to be confused the
more confused I get, the more un-cat I become. It feels like my

memories are collapsing forwards, shortening my history till all I have is an image of a dead Apricots. There must be a point to this besides horror. I wish Giant was still here. Or here in a different way. He is here as food now because I have nothing else to eat. Occasionally a mouse will emerge from a crack and I'll eat it, much to the Raccoon's howling dismay. The raccoon apparently dies for several hours a day only to resurrect into an angrier, bushier raccoon.

**

Let me try it again. This time on the curtains. There is no sound like the sound of the Mourning Dove. Aside from, of course, the sounds of other Mourning Doves, and perhaps even owls, except their noises make me go flat and pee. These sounds remind me continuously of the day my sister died. It was cold, and I was asleep some place in the forest house, maybe the scratched-up chair, and the wind moved stuff around outside which I observed through the window. It is cold so this must have been close to now, because it is still cold, colder even. I made some observations about the nature of this movement, namely how grass was all grass but also pieces of grass. Then I maybe saw wings out the window or from the porch and a thing called 'red' which, as far as I can tell, is something grey. These wings that I, maybe, saw made me sad because Apricots was dead. From a tree an Owl went *hoo*, which is confusing because it is so similar to the sound that a Mourning Dove makes. And the bats moved like an army of the dead.

**

The owl visits me and it is a strange and unnatural thing with the face of a giant. It waits on the other side of the screen window, which is the only open window, eyes heavy and large, one the full moon and the other a crescent. A color I cannot see bleeds from its moon eyes and fills the sky. There is a *hooing*. It is the color of my blood. There is a *hooing*. The color of 'red.' There is a *hooing* and it is 'flu.' I know this and see this only with the owl's harmful stare. So still, it remains so still. My cat-self is withering. Apricots speaks from its stomach, through its frozen incorrect face and tells me that it is alive, very very alive. She tells me that I have been incorrect about the extent of the world. That I am becoming more cat, not less. In the distance the deep green trees stand up and move, covering each other into a bushy wall, and everything is soundless, and the sky is 'red' and there is the sound of the Mourning Dove *cooing* in and out, in and out, and they really are the same sounds.

***

Before Giant made his head explode, he did us the kindness of giving us all the bats. It was the night after he buried his children, and Apricots and I were killing light bugs in the tall grass. So many light bugs! Giant was watching us from the porch, where he sat hugging his knees and rocking and I meowed at him to see if he wanted to kill some bugs too—but he didn't. The darkness grew less bright and the bats came to eat the bugs away from us. We tried to catch and kill them for doing so, and Giant finally showed some interest because he went into the house and came back out with the long metal tube he'd later use to blow the top of his head off. His shotgun. He sat down with a bottle of special water that made him cross-eyed and proceeded to blast heavy fire into the moving night above us making many, many dead bats. This is a memory I want to hold onto. Apricots in the darkness, eyes bright and yellow and in awe of all the bats falling dead around her, one ear flattened, happy and surprised at something, because she was never happy or surprised by anything. She used to stand in the driveway on moonless nights, seeing everything, confident in her cloak of darkness. "It's very, very alive," she would say, referring to the humming night like it was some big animal. I did not know then that it was an animal.

***

This is getting more difficult. I've done this so many times now and I am missing the point of why I am doing it. This lack. This lack feeling. I scratched it into the sofa and the ottoman and the curtains and everything and I feel time running out. To remember the feeling. To make the right tombstone for this death story, which is the only important one. Once there was a cat named Benni and a cat named Apricots. Who were they again? They were me. Benni. Benni the cat. The cat who is here. Right now. Hurry. Hurry Benni.

***

There is no sound like the sound of Mourning Dove. One time when I heard it my sister died. It was the *hooing* that reminded me. It was my sister dying that made me remind me.

Makes me remind me. I was in the house when it happened. I was asleep or maybe awake. A bird. A bird that went *hoo*.

***

What is my first memory of being cat? Was I cat before? I must have been something before. Did I have a parking lot life? Perhaps life only starts with a first memory. I was looking at Giant and Giant was holding me and I fit in his hands and he was saying words at me over and over and then I understood one of them. Benni. That is my first memory of being cat. And then I learned that Benni was me because Giant would say it and look at me when he said it, and then I saw myself in the shiny silver and when I moved, I realized that it was I, it was Benni.

Giant had smaller people in the house, and they also called me Benni and taught me words and sprayed me with the bottle for doing things I learned not to do and laughed when I tried to kill yarn. One day, I woke up without balls. Was sad and missed balls. One day, I was cleaning my penis and Giant and his small giants laughed and said it looked like a tic-tac and called me Mr. tic-tac. One day, Giant took us away in the night to a cabin in the forest and his children were quiet and scared and wailed for their mother. And they listened to the bright picture box, which is filled with things that cannot be caught, and it said that everyone else was dying very fast because of 'flu,' because of 'urgent flu.' Giant's happy face and eagerness to go on walks was different from his terrified children. They woke up very hot, and the hearts in their chests made whispering noises and I sat on their chests and tried to show them what a heart was supposed to sound like with its *thump thump thump* so they could fix theirs, but Giant kept yelling at me to, "Get off of them!" Then they were dead and Giant tried to hang himself from the ceiling fan but was too fat and fell to the ground and cried. For days he cried. Then he made his head explode.

And then Apricots got eaten by an owl and a raccoon trapped me away from all my bats.

***

Time makes hunger. Giant with ears and fingers and face all gone. I tried to protect face because face made me feel safe and warm and called me Benni when it was living, but shoe stealing raccoon wanted very much to eat the face and is bigger and can kill me. Shoe Raccoon is getting violent, did not appreciate my attempt to kill it. Soon I will have to leave. Have eaten through the screen window. Very painful. Very bloody. When we first came here Apricots and Benni crawled under the porch and killed all the mice babies! What fun! All the wriggling, squeaking babies, their grey hot flesh in our teeth.

***

There is story all around me, scent-scratches that speak in head whispers. Once there was a cat named Benni. A cat named Apricots. Once there was 'red.' Is familiar. But I cannot make enough pictures in my head. Mind can see mice and birds and grass and smells and know when to go flat or kill the small things but does not know Benni. Does not know cat. But familiar. The ideas of Benni are all around, scratched and scented. I meow at them and they do not meow back. What do I understand? There used to be a Benni. Then Benni started to go away, was taken away by a thing that went *hoo*. Two things go *hoo*. Mourning doves and owls. Benni cat wrote a story about these *hooings*. Less long ago Benni wrote it again. Benni wrote it again. I wrote it.

Me? Benni.

I move fast. Benni moves fast. There is one last thing to say while I remember. Must get it down before too late. Before I meet the owl. Must hold it in head. What it was all for. I know it now! Quickly! Through the screen window, through the hole that cuts and bloodies me, claws to pull me back to this dead place. I'll scratch it under the porch where we killed all the mice and mice babies and then I won't know how I got there. And then I'll roam and roam and never come home. The one thing that ever mattered. The point to death and life stories. Benni loved Apricots! Benni loves Apricots!

***

The night has smell-sound. Small things move in the bright dark. I see them and taste them. I am flat body. I crawl. I am crouched body. I pounce and eat a small thing, feeling it wiggle and die on my teeth. A possum comes and I am large body, big and black and something to be feared. I am soft in the grass and the grass is wet and smells deep. Trees whisper and I listen, tasting and seeing what they say, and it is very, very alive.

Behind me, wind beating, mad angry shape. Quick! I go flat body! But no, it's already here, sharp talons in my neck! For a moment I am away from the grass, in the wind. But no, I am big body! Bigger than Apricots. Who?

I fall, leaving pieces of me behind. Who? I run as flat body for place to hide. Who? There is a *hooing* and I am paws up, claws in feathers, anger in my teeth. Once there was a cat named Benni. Sharpness cuts my belly, cuts Benni's belly, a beak digging for his heart. I hear her. Yes! Yes! I remember! A voice leaks into my open body, vibrating from the bird's hungry mouth.

Haha silly owl! You think you are 'flu.' Dig all you like, that isn't where my heart is. I've hidden it far, far away. But I know where yours is. Here, let me show you.

SWITCHBACK JACK 1: THE LEGEND OF SWITCHBACK JACK

Excuse me. Yes, excuse me. This seat taken? No? It is? I'm going to take it anyway. It's my stomach. Don't look at it. Haven't seen you around. Which means you're not for long. Am I right? Of course I am. I know why you're here, young guy like you. You're here for the mountain man. The killer in the woods, Switchback's own Switchback Jack. Sap for blood, roots for veins. Bet you're a podcaster. All you kids are podcasters. Except for mine. My kid's a senator. What's that? No, I can't tell you which one, not if you want me on the record. Look, I'm not going to beat around the bush, not going to waste your time or mine. You buy, I talk. I don't do anything for free on principle. It's how I got rich. And let me tell you now, everything you've heard is a lie. Switchback Jack, he's real, but he's also not real. The true story, the one that eats the others, it's a trilogy. It's also about how I came to be the world's best dad. And like most horror stories, it's really a love story. Now get yon barman to pour me an amber and I'll switch the lights on for you.

Every eight years I scare my son. And I do mean scare. I mean living daylights. It's probably the most thoughtful decision I've ever made as a parent, certainly the most entertaining. And it's not like it's an easy thing to do. I mean, first go around it was, he was eight and all I had to do was surprise him with a corpse while hiking, but I'm getting ahead of myself. I'll get into the specifics in a second. It's all in the specifics really, parenting, being a good dad. You've got to have games, some #parentgoals if you want to reach kids at their level. That's why I invented Switchback Jack, that's why I'm probably father of the year every year, running unopposed. I'll never write a book on it, I mean it would ruin the mystique and I might be liable for some things, but I could, and the world would probably be a better place.

Like all the best ideas it started with a ghost story. I wasn't a local back then, it was before I retired, but we had a lake house right here in Switchback, VA, old family place. It was the last week of October, Halloween season, and we were up for the weekend. I was poking the coals around in the grill, watching them die, kind of hypnotized, and my son, I can't tell you his real name so let's call him Jackson, he's doing that thing kids do when they've got energy and you're only paying maybe a quarter of attention to them. You know? Tackling you around the knees a little bit, asking you dumb shit about pinecones or whatever. And he was eight, so man were those questions stupid and coming fast.

So, like I said I was doing my best to tune him out, watching the coals die, sparing glances every now and then at the mountains, their outline jagged red against deep blue, sun dying behind them, darker shades of navy and purple growing heavy up above. And I got that lonely feeling you get when the world hits you with its size. I started thinking about my own dad, how we'd come up here when I was a kid and he'd tell me stories from the other side of the fire, flame flickering between us, soot and shadow casting him like some holy man. Let me tell you, my old man could spin yarn with the best of them, till the cancer pulled it out of him. He'd tell me stories about killers, about mountain mad men. And when he held court, I could see his creations lurking in the dark fringes of the wood, these make-believe hermits standing stark against the trees, armed to the teeth with bloodstained pickaxes and hooks for hands. That fear was a kind of magic, one that I felt an instinctual need to pass on.

I must've been zoning out for a minute or so, staring out into the dusk, into that nostalgia, because next thing I know Jackson's pinching my thigh, eyes welling with little boy concern, you know, because I'm zonking. And then it hit me, the words, the beginning of the ghost story, appearing in my mind like they weren't even mine, something floated from the dark side of those kindling mountains, whispered from my father's thin lips all those years ago.

"Every eight years comes Switchback Jack," I murmured, soft and haunted, because I felt haunted.

"What?" Jackson said, whimpering, scared and getting more so. It's a great feeling, knowing your child is scared, that you can just lay a paw on their shoulder and make it go away, that or drive the feeling home, just a little.

I rode the moment, felt like the right thing to do. So much of parenting is feel. An owl called and I noticed how quiet the world had become. I could hear my wife Joan turning the pages of her Ruth Ware book over on the porch. My boy swallowed down a sob and I could hear the wet descent of his unripened Adam's Apple.

"Dad?" Jackson said, little bit of that sob popping back up, because he'd never seen me like that, didn't know what it meant.

"Oh nothing," I said, swiveling my eyes to him, putting some ruefulness into my voice, a little madness. "Nothing," I reiterated and smiled through my teeth, laying a hand and rubbing the knotty muscles in his neck. That's how it started. Fuck, I'm getting goosebumps all over again.

That night I didn't sleep. Couldn't sleep. Because I had this name. This idea. Switchback Jack. Switchback Jack. And I had my son's face right behind my eyes, that scared, dewy look he was wearing. And I knew I could do something with it, that I could pull off that little boy mask and replace it with something else. Switchback Jack. Switchback Jack. The name was becoming a heartbeat, pushing me back to those campfires, that tall-tale fear that left me drooling with wonder. Might be I wanted to experience it again, only this time from the outside, as the magic man on the other side of the fire. But a part of it was love. I wanted my son to have the same formations I did. To know the same mystique. Isn't that part of parenting? Taking what's good about you and cramming it into your offspring, turning them into you. I needed him to know that only half the world was made of light, and with it, only half the possibilities. That a tiny dose of evil, darkness is the right amount, could do wonders.

His mom, bless the woman, was into that new age parenting crap: don't yell at your kids, don't criticize your kids, don't spank your kids, don't invent murderous mountain men to scare your kids. So yeah, I took matters into my own hands. I called up my old AA buddy Tom Leary who was living as a handyman up near Woodstock and I told him I wanted to do something special for my son. And he was all like, "Oh yeah what's that?" And I told him, "Well I want to create a fictitious mountain killer and scare him a bit."

"Oh yeah?" he said.

"Yeah," I said.

"Whaddya need?" He went.

And I said, "Well I'm going to need a dead body and not that many questions."

Tom Leary, bless that man, what he wouldn't do for a hundred dollars and a bottle of wild turkey.

We ended up borrowing Leary's uncle from the mortuary two days before he was going to be shown. I had to spend eight hundred to grease things along, but I was doing okay that way. I told Joan I had some business on the golf course and drove up to Woodstock to get a look at the body. Let me tell you, the guy was perfect, kind of a guy who leaves the birth canal holding a coal shovel: around sixty, long silver beard, these big, gnarled hands the size of softballs, ice-blue eyes all fogged up with death and cataracts. Everybody hated him so we had some leniency regarding how we treated his body, seeing as the showing was likely to be a no-show. Leary had some resistance here, despite the cauliflower ears the old man had given him, there had been a sort of paternal affection between the two. I'd like to say that I didn't have to do some coercing to control the situation, but hey, I'm an alpha type of guy. If anything, Leary's sadness inspired me a little. I realized, dead uncle had to be more than just a crazy hermit. There had to be tragedy and vengeance and some deep, deep brutalization. So, I asked Leary if there was any way we could have roots growing out of the nose and eyes. I almost lost Leary at this point, so I gave him another hundred. Then I asked if he could maybe have a hook for a hand and Leary said, "Jesus Christ, Mike," but another hundred made that problem go away too. Let me tell you this now, money can make a lot of things break in your favor.

All things settled, we got the eyes out with a spoon and the hand off with a circular Leary used for fencing work, not too much blood to speak of seeing as how everything had been congealed and embalmed. The hook was a bit hard to source but eventually we settled on a gnarled piece of rebar instead which, while less functional than a hook, matched the whole Swamp Thing aesthetic better. It's like I used to tell my son, back before he was a senator and still needed telling, keep an open mind and the path finds you.

So, we had this body and we had it for maybe two days before we had to get the eyes back in, so I went about setting the atmosphere. I made sure Jackson caught me staring into the woods every so often, real haunted like, like there was something out there eating away at my peace of mind. I got short at dinner a few times, so as to eat away at his, just a little. As a parent you never want to give your children complete peace of mind, it makes them complacent.

Next morning, I woke the kid just before sunrise, sat on the foot of his bed and massaged his foot.

"Hey kiddo. How 'bout a hike with your dad," I said.

He groaned and turned away, so I took the opportunity to prime the pump so to speak. I told him how there was this mountain I used to climb with his grandpa, a beautiful place at the summit where the blackened skeleton of a burned-down lodge had collapsed in on itself, and a waterfall gurgling nearby like the mountain was murmuring a eulogy. When he still didn't get up, I gave him a hundred bucks, which to an eight-year-old is like a fucking gold bullion. So yeah, that did the trick.

Of course, we never made it up the mountain, not even sure which mountain it was. I've never climbed a mountain in my life. That wasn't part of the plan. We only had to get a quarter of the way up maybe, long enough for Leary to get dead uncle impaled on the tree we had picked out. My explicit instructions were to make it look like the corpse was, 'of the tree,' if that made any sense, which of course it didn't as Leary, bless his departed soul, had all the imagination of a pufferfish.

Anyway, I took Jackson to the mountain path, you know it might've just been a utility passage for the dam and made sure to let him lead the hike so I could vanish a few times to stoke his abandonment fears. While we walked, I continued to butter him up, told him how I once hiked the mountain by moonlight on a dare, how I was lucky that Switchback Jack hadn't found me and shoved roots through my eyes and into my frontal lobe. This of course went over about as well as you can expect. Jackson stopped and gave me a nice little Bugs Bunny eye-pop. Christ, his eyes got big, could've driven a snowplow through those pupils.

I put an arm around him and laughed his fear off, nudged him further up the trail to make him feel like he was losing control, just a little. You never want your kids to feel fully in control. Anyway, I told him that I was just joking, explained that Switchback Jack was just a local legend, some spooked up nonsense about a gold rusher driven mad by voices in the forest. I put in some details about roots thick as dog tales coiling under and bursting through skin, febrile wounds frosted with sap, organs calcified and ejected from the body through orifices to make room for the malformed tree biology forming within, roots for eyes etc. You know, the fun stuff. I added a little tragedy of-course, every good ghost story needs it, that bit about Switchback Jack being a poor Swede doing all he could for his family, trudging up and down Switchback Mountain, panning gold till his hands froze, frostbite killing his fingers to the nubs. How he'd continually get swindled out of his plots by the tougher men, forcing him deeper into the heart of the mountain where forest juju ran evil and thick. I don't want to brag but I got Jackson halfway to a panic attack, and with little to no narrative direction, no real backstory aside from the highlights. Honestly, looking back, I'm somewhat disappointed that Jackson wasn't a little more critical in his thinking. The story has a lot of holes.

Like I was saying, I had the kid close to peeing himself when Leary sent the signal, a loon call three times. I faked a phone call and speed-walked ahead, putting my finger up harshly when Jackson tried to follow, spending maybe thirty to forty minutes pretending to yell at someone that wasn't there, long enough for Jackson to get glassy-eyed and distracted, for him to start throwing pebbles back down the trail. I picked my moment and got down real slow, reverse worm-crawled into the brush, covered myself with leaves and loon called back to Leary who pressed play on a recording of my voice yelling, "Jackson! Jackson!" And boom. Trap set. Jackson turned around, found himself alone and sprinted up the mountain following my voice only to turn the bend and find Switchback Jack midway up an oak, strung up arm-spread like some butchered forest Christ. Man, I wish I could've seen the look on his face. As a parent you want to be there for all the little moments. I did get the scream, and that has to be enough.

As planned, Switchback Jack sent Jackson screaming back down the mountain taking the plan into the fourth quarter. Leary cut down the corpse and sprinted back down through the woods to head the kid off before he reached the road, setting up one of those he's behind you NO! He's IN FRONT OF YOU! gags. Classic. Can you imagine it? This fat Irish drunk lugging his dead uncle down a mountain full tilt. Of course, it didn't work, but happy accident, Leary lost control of the body and sent it tumbling down the mountain, landing right in front of, you guessed it, my son in all his pee-stained glory. Like I said, you let the path find you. I don't know if kids can have heart-attacks or whatever, but man, from what the doctors said later, Jackson might've had a really small one. He fainted outright. Which was good as it gave Leary time to catch his breath, stop crying, and drag his uncle's mutilated corpse back into the woods, leaving me there at my kid's side, ready to play hero. Man, I love it when a plan comes together. And don't worry, Jackson's heart is fine, like I said he's a senator, if anything it's stronger, like a wolf's heart, the ventricles all angry and rigid, howling at a forever moon.

HECTOR OF TROY COMMUNES WITH SCOTT NORWOOD IN THE AFTERLIFE

This is not what I expected. Not death I mean. I expected that. The way it happened, too. Me, like a fool, running in circles with that ingrate on my heels. Not the way I wanted it but, you know, I gave it a shake. Almost got him too, but that spear. Wide right. Could've sworn I had it lined up. Achilles, black against the sun, scrambling, a bow legged dog, panting, angry panting, and me, halfcocked ready to send a spear into his rage-hoarse gullet. It doesn't matter now, as he drags me into viscera around my home, but he really is a fat pig. Just fat and muscle and stupid pig brains. A thoughtless fist to grind the civilizations of the world into dust. Who would conspire to make such a thing? Gods, of course. Not that I should trend towards impiety now but... I mean... I really did a lot of things right. Didn't I? I loved my wife. I fought for my brother. My father. My people. I loved my son. Poor little Astyanax. I took my helm off when it scared you. In death, I see too much. I see the moment of decision when they chuck your fat little boy body off the wall. My son! My boy! I left you to go fight on the bloody shore knowing full well my chances. Thanks gods. I have to say. If I could have done it again, I would have spent far more of my time raving at you lot atop the wall, exposing my buttocks and farting at your holy mountain. Because here I am now, aforementioned viscera, with strange visions of the afterlife. And my son is dead, or soon my son will die.

The war does not end. It somehow expands. A giant.... amphitheater of sorts. A large green battlefield. It really does look nice. A manicured emerald to dwarf all our dusty arenas. There is a system to it. Indecipherable to me. Whoops! Bump there. Drive straight you murderous ninny! White lines with...ciphers?.... numbers?... all along both sides. If this is my eternity, I'll have time to figure it out. Gods. The people. A sea of them surrounds the fight. We've somehow multiplied in constant death. Some wine-dark, some white. Which are we? White. Yes, that seems right. Apollo appropriate. Lusty cur that one. Just ask my sister.

There's some sort of bull on our helmets. A small battalion of our boys are lined up against theirs. And look at this! The people are mingling in this gargantuan mass. White and wine-dark mixing in strangling proximity. How far in the future is this? The tongues are strange, there seem to be tiny suns all around the top of this arena...whatever this place is. Perhaps the years have rendered our eternal war into a mockery. A positive feedback loop of what's been done on my shores. See how they stop everything each minute and reset. How strange this all is. Gods, I hate you. Remember that when my fat little boy reaches you or reaches here. Maybe he'll be that brown, roundish thing the soldiers are bandying about. My little boy tossed around for eternity. You know I can't really describe the shape, it's like a melon sized...olive... but brown and pointier on both ends. Sometimes our side throws it or runs with it and sometimes the wine-dark Greeks do. By turns, I think. The goal is to move this object to the other end while the other side tries to beat you. I don't really get it. At least no one has died yet despite all the pummeling. This vision would be a lot clearer if this mongrel knew how to drive a chariot. Then he could better desecrate me. Look at him howling at my wife and father in victory. It's been two hours and he's still not bored. I wish they'd leave, no reason to watch this anymore. It's not unfaithful. I must be supremely dead at this point. All glory consumed in this singular shame.

He'd be good at this game, Achilles. As opposed to what? Landscaping painting. Or course he would be. It's not fair. What does this mean? The staccato back and forth, the screaming, and yes, laughing. Cruel gods you've crushed us into parody. I'm sure you're up there watching this self-replicating war. It's finally become fun. Bastards.

And look something's happening. A skinny man is walking to the field. His shoulders are slumped. They've placed the ball at his feet. An offering? But this man is no soldier, no prince, no champion. All eyes are drawn to him, a weakling focal point for the rangy, wild minds of this comedy. We line up to defend him as he prepares to do something. There's something on his back. Something on all their backs. A different sequence of symbols. Names? How odd. Yet this man, I can sense his presence. He looks backwards in time at me. Almost sees me. Norwood.

Yes. His name. Oh, you poor bastard. He kicks the strange brown object just as the Wine-Darks bullrush. It tumbles, end over end, its destination the space between two bright yellow poles. How do I know this? Achilles is cutting me loose now, pointing to the sand where friction and ground have conspired to squish my genitals into red murk. The object is curving, fluttering in the gusting wind. Of course. Of course. The space where evil lives. The dead center that can never be struck, is not allowed to be struck. Norwood knows it. I can see it in the language of his knees. Try not to get discouraged, friend. It happens to the best of us.

WOWEE-ZOWEE (SUDDEN DEATH)

The trouble started when I heard my son's teddy bear asking for help with suicide.

Jackson was about four months old then, and I had just started being able to sleep outside the nursery, had stopped holding a spoon over his mouth to see the fog, to know that his little life hadn't been snatched away. It came over the monitor, a breeze of a voice that woke me from sleep in our darkness addled nest, a caress of sound that fluttered my lids, "Please Jack, cutting my head off should do it. You can use the kitchen scissors. And then Wowee-Zowee gone I'll be." It had the voice of a child, but the pitch was too high, and mechanical, something you'd squeeze the paw of in a toy store, a mechanical grind beneath it. And I lay there staring at the monitor, at the digital glow above the speaker, reading out the time of the world in deep luminescent green.

My wife didn't hear, at that point she was having trouble staying awake and moving on account of the fact that our bed had turned into a minor cave system. I mean that the duvet had grown, that it had enfolded her into its canyons of white depth, a mattress sinkhole that had extended down beneath her. She felt very far away from me. So, it was just me trying to wrangle

53

the situation, to somehow understand why my son's teddy was trying to introduce him to violent suicide.

When I walked into the nursery it was silent, and my son was silent, in that tomb sleep he'd been born into, unmoving, which is what scared me so much and why I'd started with the spoon. He'd never move, he'd never wriggle, never was afraid and confused at being alive.

Which, as a parent, is what you want.

Ruggles was in the crib with him, a tawny curl of a thing with black bead eyes, a survivor of several goes through the washing machine. Overhead the sea creature mobile turned ever so slightly, like a spirit had gone through it. He was just a little bundle there, in his crib prison, and if I hadn't known, hadn't trusted, I would have still been there with the spoon. But you have to trust. You have to.

I took Ruggles with me into the den, which is really the kitchen, we had a two bedroom. And I sat there undoing the knots in his fur like I was an ape and he was my ape child. He'd been my teddy for so long. Until Jackson. My mom had given him to me, I was a little attached. It's hard to leave behind a thing you've named, harder still to kill it. Is that weird? Doctor Geronimo implied it might have been weird. I sat there grooming him and I asked him why he wanted to end it. And why Jackson? Why a little baby instead of his oldest friend?

And what he said, in that little grinding voice like an out of breath wind-up toy, was that it was because he was afraid, afraid all the time. Because he couldn't be there all the time, and when you weren't there all the time anything, really anything, could happen. Just thinking about it had wrung him ragged.

And so I said to him, because I knew where he was coming from, that maybe he should give me a specific example. He told me about this guy who'd had a kid, who was so worried all the time, so worried that he'd sleep next to the crib each night with a spoon in his hand, checking every few minutes to make sure the kid was breathing. Because he loved his son so much. So, he wasn't there when a blood clot made its way into his wife's brain.

And she died as he stood on guard in the other room. Because anything can happen.

So, I cut his head off with the kitchen scissors, because who'd want to live through a thing like that.

THE GENEALOGY OF POPS

The first thing I saw was blue. The second thing I saw was Pops. The first thing I feared was God. That's how I learned to order the universe. My first memory of a place was Boat-Raft-City. It's a pretty cool place. Everything's pretty alright. I mean it's small. But that's the deal. We only live in small communities now. It's considered best for everybody. Stronger individuals. Everybody knows everybody. A healthier zeitgeist. Less schizophrenic living.

We live on a boat. Or rather, more precisely, on boats. Correction. Like, we live on boats that are tied together. So, like a raft. Or a collection of boats, that on a macro scale operates like a large raft, and, on a regular level, looks and operates like a boat. On a personal, scale I live on a boat called the *Haphazard*. It's kind of like the ass of the raft.

There're other dudes out there. Other people on other raft cities. But we don't talk to them. It's kind of culturally forbidden on account of our unwavering need to maintain a healthy communal psyche, which would be in severe jeopardy among the presence of outsiders. Outsiders whose thinking can simply not be accounted for. Like one time, I saw a boat of outsiders-whose-thoughts-couldn't-be-accounted-for throwing babies overboard their ship. Which made my throat tight. I'm glad we don't do that here. And we do some weird stuff. So yeah, we don't socialize. I mean we trade. Sometimes. But, we never socialize when we do it. Pops said that's why guns and armpits were invented: so we don't have to socialize. Socializing and unhealthy zeitgeists were the reason the Old World ended. Now we just put supplies in lifeboats and hope for honesty.

Back to the babies. The thing about the babies is population control is super important on Boat-Raft-City. Turns out babies are super easy to make. Turns out you and me and everybody can have a hand in the making of babies, but too many babies on Boat- Raft-City is bad for resources, which creates food and water shortages, which creates unhappy people, which creates an unhealthy zeitgeist, which leads to wild tribal violence and sometimes, confusingly, even more babies. So we control babies. The only time banging is technically allowed is under an Elder Supervised Procreation Session or ESPS for short. I'm a little uncomfortable in an ESPS on account of performance anxiety issues and an atavistic sense that an unknown Elder is checking out my butt. Also, when the participants finish, the Elders do a little clap and sigh wistfully.

Unsanctioned bonking is a big no-no, but we do it anyway. The Elders try to catch sweaty teenagers off guard but it's a hard thing to prove if they don't witness any penetration. I'm a sweaty teenager and a conscientious objector to the policy. If it were up to me, I'd be bonking left and right. Personally, I've bonked a sum total of one and a half times. The one time was an ESPS with Lilly Simms. This was, to be honest, pretty much a brokered exchange. I'd speared a bonkers marlin fish that day and brought it to Elder Simms as a sort of let-me-pork-your-daughter-gesture. What ensued was the best, and only, ESPS of my life with a clap at the end and everything. The general consensus is, and was, that I'm radically beneath Lilly. In that particular instance I was.

The half time I bonked was just for fun and I remember it much better. Lilly and I were in an overturned lifeboat and even though it was dark, the water shone emerald with luminescent algae. I remember how flecks of green peppered Lilly's skin like stars in a cosmic swirl, her body lithe and barely suggested in a sea of black motion, a human constellation. For me the moment was seminal. Lilly made me finish in the water. Which was painful because salt got in my dick-hole. So it only counts half. But I'd do it again, I'd definitely do it again.

So, as I said we monitor procreation. But still, it's a problem. There's simply not much to be done about it. I mean people try. We have some pretty strict anti-bonking policies around here. Like for instance, compulsive masturbating is generally encouraged and considered polite. It's not uncommon to walk through the fish market and see multitasks browsing fish and tugging at the same time. I don't eat at the fish market. Pops didn't either. He found it morally incorrect and unsanitary. Pops told me when he was my age, back before the world got blown up and flooded, he compulsively masturbated in front of a computer screen. Apparently, this was not only the proper way to masturbate compulsively, but also the correct use for computers. Computers don't work anymore. I've tried to compulsively masturbate to one but all I see is myself.

Pops hated computers. He called them lie machines. He said they were almost as bad as television, which he called a sentient lie machine. He told me he was pretty sure that at one point in his life, his TV had most assuredly moved places in the night and tried to kill him with toxic visuals. One toxic visual was this thing called porn. According to Pops, porn was a kind of third-person-fucking-magic-window. If you looked into it, you could see beautiful people with large wangs and firm titties compulsively fuck for money. Pops said it was pretty similar to an Elder Supervised Procreation Session minus the clapping.

Pops used to be an Elder. He relinquished his position because he got tired of working for, 'The Man.' This was a lie. He quit because people hated him. He quit because some of the other Elders bandied around the suggestion of throwing him and me off Boat- Raft-City for sedition, which would have been bad for us and nutritional for God. This is how he became an outcast. This is how I came to be beneath Lilly Simms.

Anyhow, Pops blamed the destruction of our intended life on Earth on lie machines, because lie machines had made the world increasingly absurd. Lie machines made it incredibly difficult for people to rationalize their experiences and created a communal dissociative mindset. Everything went bonkers. Everything reached and surpassed a bonkers threshold wherein bonkers became confused with normalcy. Then bonkers caught fire and decided to burn the village, so to speak. I asked my Pops what he saw on the lie machine that made him so sure of this theory. He said he only remembered one thing: it was a story about wonderful smoothies that could somehow make women incredibly thin and give them orgasmic pleasure all at the same time. In the story, several women danced half- naked and made orgasm faces while they drank the seemingly magic beverages. I asked my father what this meant philosophically; he shook his head in a sad way. He was a sad dude. I think he suffered from existential depression. God ate him. He's not around anymore.

God. God is a horrific, gigantic sea creature who chases Boat-Raft-City around the Atlantic and tries to eat us at night. Between the hours of midnight and dawn, God uses its approximately five-thousand suctioned tentacles to grope us away from existence. God has roughly three hundred red spinal protrusions that carve through the water like tower-high swords in a v-pattern. God has a biblical number of blowholes on its back that eject a million streams of bioluminescent algae thousands of yards into the air at the precise moment the sun rises over the horizon, signaling the end of his rampage. This is the most majestic and life affirming vista in the history of existence. I know because Pops told me, and he did a lot of acid while visiting someplace called Yosemite.

We eat algae. We eat a metric ton of algae. It's kind of our spiritual contract with Giant-Fish-Monster-God. But frankly, and I mean no disrespect to algae, it's pretty baseline awful. As soon as God dives for the day we paddle out in canoes and scoop up buckets full of algae to painfully consume. We don't need to eat the algae anymore, on account of late-stage fishing skills, but we do it as a reminder that life used to be mega-crazy, and we should totally appreciate it not being so anymore. The Elders describe the eating and the puking and the crying as an act of humiliating contrition, of shaming ourselves for the things that lead us here. There's a chant that happens when we do this, it goes: "Shame! Shame! Shame on human progress!"

I remember there was this one guy who, in the middle of algae gathering, told everyone on the raft that God's algae was actually this thing called manna, and that he'd read about it in a book somewhere. He was very forceful on this issue, and not big on shaming human progress, and at one point bit somebody. The Elders said that line of thinking and that kind of biting, was perhaps not super-fantastic. They threw him off the boat. Sharks ate him.

After the shark-eating, the Elders convened us and told us how important it was not to treat or think about God or ourselves as anything special. They told us to lump him in with boring, every day occurring things like the sun and the moon. They told us to think of God as just another fantastic, but completely expected, natural phenomenon that simply took its turn telling us what to do. Pops shook his head when he heard this. He spent the next four hours contemplating the movements of a cloud. He never scooped algae. We weren't very popular for it, but my Pops never wanted to be popular.

He wanted to be alone and stare.

While God shooting glowing green lava into the heavens is fantastic and life affirming beyond measure, it is for the most part a harrowing terror. God is also the sole reason mankind is alive, on account of it rising up from the irradiated seas and recreating our atmosphere through the spouting of oxygen spewing algae. The atmosphere was gone on account of the F-bombs. F-bombs were kind of like portable infernos that not only killed everything but also revoked the atmosphere, turning it into a thin mist that made living barely possible. Apparently, the term F-bomb was some sort of joke. Apparently, when mankind invented anything permanently-word-destroying a small amount of ironic humor was necessary to validate the process.

Sometimes I think God's ironically funny. Sometimes when God sleeps its rolling slumber pushes us in the direction of land. We get to see the burned husks of cities rising in the distance like little black fingers. So yeah, we begrudgingly put up with God. It was God's algae that returned oxygen to the atmosphere after we scorched it away. It's a kind of symbiosis. We take turns eating each other.

Pops' friend Ken was mega-way-into God. He had what Pops referred to as a theological obsession. Ken wasn't from Boat-Raft-City originally. He just sort of showed up one day in a sailboat filled with harpoons and heartbreakingly beautiful sketches of whales. We let him onboard on account of him continually throwing harpoons at us while cursing in Japanese. He was a wacko.

Pops and Ken got along great on account of them sharing the same form of existential depression. They couldn't communicate verbally on account of the language barrier, but they could grunt and ponder clouds with tremendous synchronization. This trait made them useless and extensively unpopular. I'm kind of extensively unpopular too, on account of the fact that Pops was my Pops and Ken was his bestie.

The thing I remember about Ken was his life and his death, which is kind of an expansive thing to remember, but also really simple. All Ken ever did was hurl harpoons at God while cursing in Japanese, gesticulating wildly at a whale sketch in reprobation.

Despite Ken's best efforts, God continued to eat whales with what can be considered reckless abandon, which in turn only fueled Ken's spear-throwing. This was pretty much Ken's only skill set, aside from the creation of heartbreakingly beautiful whale sketches, which, in my opinion, are pretty great. I've got a couple hanging in the *Haphazard* today. They help me with my existential depression.

Sometimes, Ken talked about his home through pictographs and grunts. He was like Pops. A man from a different time. A child from a different world, some higher dimension where water and monsters weren't arbitrary conditionals. A place called Japan. A place that had apparently spent millions of dollars predicting the ascension of God and practiced fighting it on a daily basis via Lie Machines. The practice didn't pay off. They all died.

Ken's daughter died in an F-Bomb blast. She was scorched away by a mad wind of fire. After her death, Ken could recognize the spot where she had been cremated, her anti-self. He lay down next to this anti-her and in a day or so a great wave came and throttled him out to sea. He would have died if not for the whale that ate him. The whale imparted rare earth knowledge upon him and ejected him out into the New World. I suspect Ken might have been a Lie Machine.

Ken's dead now. One day he ran out of harpoons to throw at God and found himself to be the next nearest object. There wasn't a moment of hesitation. No, 'Hey guys I'm off to suicide because I ran out of spears and my honor demands it,' which would have been nice for me, although culturally foreign.

Given how thoroughly dedicated Ken was to his obsession, I could have understood. It was especially sad for Pops. I think watching Ken gave Pops the idea. I've never quite got over that.

As I said, Pops was a sad guy. He was also a wacko guy. But he was pretty alright. I think his problem was he had exhausted himself in his prior life, which made him cranky and aloof. Every morning he woke and expected to be back there, back among things he couldn't replace. I think there's a point in life where new things start to crush you. I think an essential part of Pops got crushed. He had managed to repair that part a little, till it worked just enough, but it would never be shiny again.

It was in the beautiful hours that he only ever woke up from his stupor. In the light drenched mornings and dusks, the moments before and after God's bliss and carnage, I would see him walk the decks of Boat-Raft-City in bewilderment, searching the swirling horizon for something. He looked like a befuddled prophet; his silver hair wild like a starched thunderbolt. In these dazes, he would respond to no one. Not even me. Sometimes children would throw fish heads at him. I remember following him around, picking up fish heads and throwing them back. Sometimes he would stand on the bow of our boat and yell esoteric things at God as God stirred awake in the red glamour of the setting sun, primed to embark upon another night of feasting on the bounty of the sea: dolphins, whales, and people. Sometimes he'd just stare out into the distance. If there wasn't any distance to be stared at, he would stare at some indoor object and act like it was distance. One time, he looked at a boot for three hours. After two hours I moved the boot, and he didn't say anything. So I moved it back. After the third hour he asked me if I'd seen the boot moving, which I had because I had moved it. When I remember this moment, his ponderous head heaving left and right from the boot to me, I see him as an animal. I think that's what he wanted. To be something clean and uncomplicated. Maybe that's why he jumped.

He didn't say anything. Didn't say goodbye. But he saw me. And I saw him. Then he was in the water occupying the reflection of the moon. Then he was part of the carnage. One of God's arms pulled him underneath to what I can only assume were waiting jaws. To be honest with you, my world got a little smaller. I miss his ponderous head. Sometimes I have dreams where he returns to me as a wise and scarred walrus, and we talk on a great slab of ice in the middle of the sea. And there's no great Boat-Raft-City. There's no horrific sea monster dictating the current of life. There's just him and me and we only need to look at each other to exchange wide swathes of feelings. Sometimes I think my dreams are Lie Machines too.

Listen to me. I want you to understand something. This isn't a bad life. It's not an unhappy life. Things go on. People fall in the water and drown. Things go on. People jump overboard at night and let God eat them. Things go on. People grow old and die in their beds. Things go on. And between all the things-going-on, there's some love, some hate, some fear, some hope. Like, for instance, I hope to spear another choice marlin so I can pork Lilly Simms again in an ESPS. And, if I do a good job porking her and everyone's okay with us making a new person, I think that would be pretty great. There'd be room for a lot of love there and I could always talk about Pops. And we could go under the lifeboat again and I wouldn't mind my dick-hole hurting.

Aside from Lilly, I've got the *Haphazard* to myself. Sometimes people forget that I'm even here. On those days, when there's no knock on my cabin, no fishing to be done, I slip out and ride my little boat. It's an old thing, a smoothed and waxed canoe with a little diesel engine at the back. I give it a few pulls and stand up. Then I carve the blue. I feel the speed of all life. I feel myself come apart at the seams as all the lies that make me a Lie Machine spread out into vapor. Something clean and uncomplicated. And I think about Pops. And we have nonverbal communications, like a song. And when I hear it I go faster, put down everything I have. And when the algae blooms, borne upwards from the body of that great fish, I can feel our dead communicating. In the effervescent dawn, I let the glowing- green rain down upon me and test my luck, knowing how I'll die. I only hope it looks beautiful, my home floating in the distance, lit up and twinkling like a colony of stars, existing for the first and last time.

SWITCHBACK JACK 2: THE LAKE HOUSE MASSACRE

Another beer. You know, make it two. And no, I don't have a problem. No fucking way. I'm retired. I can die how I want. My son's a senator.

Okay, the dead teenagers. Let me start by saying, it's not like I wanted there to be dead teenagers. But if you want to do things right, you gotta break some eggs, and sometimes, those eggs just happen to be other people's children. And, it's not like I expressly told Leary to start killing people. That mostly was his decision, and to be honest, he was in a pretty bad way around then, bless his soul, so it wasn't really his decision either. But it's not like I don't take responsibility. I take all the responsibility. Especially for how well my senator son has turned out, which might not have happened had he not gotten the confidence boost of killing someone with an onboard motor. Were you not paying attention to the first part? And it's not like I didn't lose anything, Leary was a dear friend of mine. I hope he's gone someplace where he can kill as many teenagers as he likes. But let's be serious here, the guy was just waiting for an excuse to go apeshit. I mean who sells the corpse of their dead uncle for booze money? Guy might as well have been Jack Torrence. Did I give him a push? Maybe. But he fell the fuck over on his own, let the record show that.

Point is, when my son turned sixteen, Switchback Jack came back. Like I said, every eight years. Like a trust fund, only instead of cash, I give my son intense character building. Of course, I gave him money as well. I guess I should say he inherited it, as I'm legally dead. I know I don't look it, but I used to be very, very wealthy. I still am, but most of it is tied up in offshore accounts and the Republican Party. Money's the most important fucking thing on the planet. But you've got to teach your children how to use it, else they'll wind up pouring it into coffee shops and God knows what other kinds of shenanigans.

Like I was saying, Jackson was sixteen and turning into a little shit. Most of it was normal teenager stuff: the moping, the nightmares, the masturbation. Again, his mother was so, so soft on him. He had this pathetic streak; things would just scare the hell out of him and he'd go to pieces. Shadows, loud noises, trees, old bearded men. You name it. He'd have these night terrors and piss the bed. Yet when he was awake, he'd be cock of the walk. A real in-your-face brat. Fuck you, dad. You can't buy my love, dad. When do I get to stay with mom? I would've been okay with the attitude if it was for real. But he wasn't pure alpha. It was all an act to cover up the bed pissing. Truth was, by age sixteen, Jackson was chickenshit, and I wasn't about to have chickenshit for a son.

So, what did I do? I gave old Tom Leary a call and we got things working again. Granted he didn't have a phone anymore, so I had to go visit him in the dilapidated shack he'd started living in after our adventure eight years prior. Something about what we'd done hadn't set well with him. I don't know, guys like Tom, they're fuckups no matter how much you take care of them. Poor bastard, he fell to his knees and cried when he opened the door and found me standing there. I can have that effect sometimes. People, they just love me. Sometimes it's my stomach though. I said don't look at it.

I had to get Tom drunk again to get him to cooperate. It wasn't hard, I mean, he wasn't well, the interior of the cabin could tell you as much. He had these bark masks all over the walls, these sap crusted hollow-eyed monstrosities, blank slit mouths. Horrific stuff. They sell imitations in the gift shops now. So, he wasn't well. And he wanted me to leave, which I knew he didn't really mean, so I freshened his coffee with just a little bit of whiskey. And maybe some PSYOP grade acid I copped from a fed buddy. That did the trick. We were back on the same side again.

In retrospect maybe I should've had some understanding about what was haunting him. You ever hear that saying, 'life imitates art?' Well, something like that was going on with Tom. I think on some level I was impressed with what he'd done with my idea. He'd gone in a sui generis kind of direction with it, someplace I could never go. Well until I did. I've always been more of a director. Needless to say, I was impressed, I think, and also maybe a little possessive and vengeful. So, if I sidestepped certain inconvenient truths well, sue me, only good luck finding my address.

The plan was simple. A game of hide and seek with teeth. Jackson was coming up to the Vermont house that weekend with some of his friends: cheerleader girlfriend, star running back, a couple of the losers he sold drugs with. I wasn't necessarily okay with the drug selling but I was very okay with the enterprising nature of it. Remember what I said about dark possibilities, selling drugs is as good a way to get into Harvard as any. It might've been the only thing Jackson did back then that wasn't chickenshit.

Point being, Jackson was going up there to have some fun and when that fun reached a peak, once the fucking and the drugging and the whatnot was really going, Leary was going to stalk out of the bushes like the Vorhees express and scare the lot of them, maybe even choke one or two out, drag 'em into the darkness real gentle like. Now I believe I communicated this last part very clearly, no one was supposed to die, I was and am currently not interested in dead teenagers. But unfortunately, maybe on some subconscious level, Tom Leary was very interested. That or the acid had completely fried his mind and taken him back to the gulf. I'll admit that might've been a possibility. He passed out at some point during my primer, so maybe he didn't even hear the part about not killing anyone. Again, sort of my fault but also not completely my fault. Granted I should've seen part of it coming when I picked him up that Friday evening and he had his Switchback Jack mask on. I told him the mask wasn't necessary, even tried to take it off because it was even making me a little chickenshit, but the thing had become part of him, fused to his face with some dank mixture of sap and blood. As for the sharpened rebar bolted to his hand, well, I didn't even try to take that away. If I had, I don't think you'd be buying me beer, and yes you can fill that glass up again.

I dropped Leary off about a mile from the house, I'd bought all the woods and lake surrounding the place. You never know when you might need a whole bunch of woods and lake to do stuff in. Man, he looked beautiful, this hulking misshapen thing standing at the treeline, knives of blood red sun carving the air around him, silhouetting his shape into evil depths. It gave me chills, those same campfire chills I'd been missing for so long. He looked like a thing stepped out of hell, primed for death and destruction. But he had also soiled himself in the car, so you know, you can forgive me for misreading the situation.

"Go get them," I probably said. "Terrify them to their very cores'," I probably said. "Go kill them all." I definitely did not.

The rest happened pretty much how the papers printed. There was more nudity in the movie. Leary kept the weapons embedded in the bodies so there wasn't really much mystery, to the how at least. He walked around with the cheerleader's head spiked onto the rebar till the end. That was rough. I liked her, Jackson said they were in love. But whatever. At least she went quick. Not like the stoners. Leary did one with the ceiling fan, suplexed the other lengthwise on six feet of picket fence, real tall that one. The jock got a bocce ball in each lung. Never liked him anyway. But you know, sad of course.

I'm not sure if Leary ever made a serious attempt on Jackson. He mostly battered him around with his girlfriend's head. That was when I really wanted to jump in, seeing him get clubbed unconscious like that. But that would've undermined the whole point, you know? And my son probably wouldn't be a senator. At some point you've got to let your kids fight their own battles. And Jackson did alright. After regaining consciousness, he followed Leary out into the night, found him down by the lake, sleeving branches into his intestines, yelling some nonsense about becoming one with the tree. Man, that acid must've been something else. Jackson quietly got the onboard motor from the lake boat and went about scooping out the back half of Leary's skull. Bless that poor bastard. I bring a bottle to his unmarked every anniversary of the brain scooping.

I took some photos of the moment. Night vision of course. My son like fucking Rambo, face crusted with girlfriend blood, boat motor held heavy to his stomach, becoming a man. Now that he's out in the world and I'm legally dead, that photo has become my most prized possession, my son killing his boyhood. Brings a tear to my eye. I'd like to give it to him one day, but I can't let him know that I was out there, following it all from a distance. It's his moment, not mine, his campfire bite-mark to study by firelight.

THE FUGITIVE FINDS CHRIST

Before I swing, let me tell you what rots inside me. I have spent my years running from this rope, only to find that I was chasing its noose. I first felt it tighten on the isle of Iona.

It was on a rain struck midnight that I, pursued by the Protestant law that ran roughshod over Ireland, found myself before the Scottish abbey, a great lump growing moss-like from the knotted hills of that stony place, lightning splitting the grey of the sky and sea as they roiled above and below, myself a small and shrouded fugitive. The monastery was dark but for a candled window, wherein I saw the shape of a great cat watching my approach, shadowed head embedded with the sinister glow of a single amber eye. Let me tell you, the devil is certain, it is a one-eyed cat named Cormac within whose belly lies the remains of my smallest toe. I knocked upon the door, the sound drowned out by the cracking fury of thunder and swelling wave. There I slept, sodden, head swimming with the banshee mewling of that strange feline drawing over me in a cloud of fever.

In the morning I was found half-dead. Unconscious, I was dragged in and tonsured by the presiding Abott Fionnlagh, a stout Benedictine Scot with a face like a snowman, button black eyes in puddled white flesh, a warty carrot for a nose. He had deduced that I was his for reformation, delivered by God's own providence to his abbey to be hung and dried in the penance of redemption. Despite his rough manner he was not unkind to me, demanding only the obedience that marked the other monks, silence and reflection, to speak only when necessary.

Though in him I sensed his own darkness, a severe single-mindedness that could exclude the world. At heart he was but a simple man, of simple tempers, a scholar whose two ambitions were faith in God and the completion of his life's work, an illuminated manuscript of the gospels in his country's own Scottish Gaelic. What his fate may have been I do not know. But I shudder to think that either heaven or hell saw fit to hollow him out.

It was from Fionlagh that I first learned my diction. He taught me to speak and spell as he did as I accompanied him around the isle in search of malachite and sulfur, the stones to powder, the roots to prune, elements that could be pulverized into dyes for his parchment foils. Together he would point out the creatures of the Isle, plants that would cure and kill, skills that have made my punishment long. He could be a storm, though, a tankard at my head if ever I spoke too often and too freely, if ever I showed myself the blackguard Irishman that I was and am, a thing no pretty talk can cover. There was an allure for him in my incivility, I was the curious equivalent of a lost savage, a spark of Christian potential to be fanned into a glow, proof that a mongrel could be made to stand upright.

I was drunk more often than not, all the Benedictines were, fresh water on the isle being rare and as like to poison as kill a thirst. We brewed constantly to stomach it, living off sweet mash and ale. I had done worse for drink and food in my belly. A roof over my head. And between Fionnlagh's teachings and the hot meals, I thought the abbey could be a home, the soft colored light that filtered through the colored glass windows a grace upon my harried shoulders, the salt air over green grass and sure grey stone a resurrection. In that holy burrow, I forgot about the puritans, the stiff winds scattering my dreams of the loch and those it held, the echoes of past mischief quieted. The spilt brains on pub floors. I was never without guilt for the protestant girl though. I never have been since I had finished with her. And I imagine it'll be that lass I see first when condemned to the pit. Mark me, there is a bone in us that longs for redemption, despite our evil, I know this as well as any Peter or Paul. Despite that, I'd taken her a thousand times over, but my regret for doing it is real. I had confused that grief for a mark in my favor, confusing goodness as a refusal to do evil. But in truth, it was the mark upon my forehead.

It was the cat that did it for me. A massive, unnatural thing, a midnight black tom as big as a collie, right eye scratched into an unseeing pulp by one of the rats that plagued the cellar, balls as big as cherries, ears tufted into downy horns above his head, a spine arched so savagely it threatened to rip from his silken hide. A perfect angel to Fionlagh and the brothers, purring for belly rubs and games of paw, stumbling into walls to prove his infirmity. But when we were on our lonesome, he showed the spirit that he was, stalking me from the shadows and rafters, one eye night-glazed and precise in the chasmal gloom. He'd watch me from the door of my cell as I tried to sleep, nibbling at my toes if ever I dozed too long, pouncing at my heels as I knelt in prayer. I wondered then, as now, what the truth of him was, something monstrous by chance or malignant by design, a witch's familiar or a soul-stealing Cait Sith? When I wasn't worked to the bone, I'd often wander the emerald curves of the island searching for proof of his origin, expecting with each crest of hillside the distant glow of the cauldron that birthed him.

Cormac's trap was a simple one, a matter of letting me drown in comfort. After I had settled myself into the monastic life, proving myself adequate to minor tasks, Cormac quit his own responsibilities, the slaughter and control of the abbey's rodent infestation. As Cormac lounged in indolence, the vermin, undeterred, took to raiding our stores with impunity. Fearing the repercussions of a rodent consuming the eucharist, Fionnlagh charged me with guarding the consecrated bread overnight.

It was a task I took on with all my earnestness, the chance to prove myself a true brother of the abbey. I could feel God's love behind the very moment, his stewardship manipulating the circumstances that would lead me to redemption, my own transubstantiation from cutthroat.

But the nights were long and I was mildly drunk at all hours. Cormac watched with dull curiosity as I lurched and wobbled to and fro across the pantry, scraping my palms bloody on the cobbled floors as I sought to grab and crush the soft little bodies that meant to steal divinity out from under us. It was a losing effort. With each hour awake, with each hour illicitly slept through, the blessed loaves grew pockmarks, culprits scampering towards crevices where they mocked me, cheeks stuffed, watching me through visionless black bead eyes.

I did not consider any of these infractions as serious, thought my task was one chiefly of spirit. Still, for nights I toiled to hide the evidence of my failure, secreting the tarnished loaves around the abbey to prevent discovery: under pews, buried at the foot of the great Gaelic cross, secreted into the chambers of the brothers or flung into the sea. I was determined to fulfill my task or to appear to do so.

Fionnlagh was satisfied, proud even, inviting me to powder the elements for his dyes. As a gift of thanks, he gave me a slender vial of indigo for use in transcribing my own thoughts, a gift that out-valued me many times over. I felt resurrected, the flesh of my own wayward past altered as promised; the thrill of a deed well-done flowed through me, imagined though the deed was. I grew slack in my stewardship of the eucharist, allowing more and more to be taken each night, occasionally feeding the pests myself. With my indigo I scrawled a small blasphemy in the corner of the pantry, a representation of the lord Christ in the form of a mouse. It was a jest, but the action had power, it had consequences.

The nights proceeded as they had. I entered a small detente with the rodents, offering them handfuls of my meals in exchange for the security of the eucharist. While they ate, I read from the volumes Fionnlagh had lent me to practice my letters: Herodotus, Plato, the great Thomas Aquinas. Reading was a skill I had a knack for. I felt my mind growing, my thoughts expanding into ideas and images I had never considered. For the first time I felt true guilt, not of the stomach but of the mind, for what I had done, what I had robbed others of, the ideas and sensibility of Italy and Europe. The opportunity to see and know that God had created far more than the dreary Isle from whence I came, offered more than the rain-soaked beatings and humpings my kind struggled in. But you see this was the punishment. To be educated out of my stupor to the point where I could understand the gravity of my sins and thus be tortured by them.

I remember them clearly, the tiny paw prints of blood that led me to Christ, to the knowledge of my character. I was roused from Aquinas's notes on Aristotle by a soft mewling, barely audible. In the corner, lapped by the inky darkness that fed on my candlelight was a congregation of mice, standing as men do in a circle, heads bent in what looked like prayer. It was from them that the noise came, an incomprehensible whisper that still haunts my restless hours. The language of angels. I went to look; I was drawn to look. I saw the tracks, a trajectory of blood-prints no larger than half my smallest nail. I looked into the rodent circle, my face bathed in the miasma of their tiny breaths and I saw a raw bundle, a newborn mouse with stigmata wounds and shoulder length, flowing hair the color of chestnut.

From behind came movement. A slow, living hiss. I turned to see the great bulk of Cormac, a thing fused to the shadows, revealed only by his malignant eye and white jaws, from which dangled the squirming body of a mouse. With a crunch the cat-thing finished his prey, depositing a tiny head onto the cobbled floor with the barest of thuds. He grinned at me, I swear to it, and unleashed a yowl that sunk through the stone and lichen of that blessed place. And I knew what he planned to do, what my negligence had allowed to happen. The Christ mouse was gone, vanished with its attendants during my vigilance, and the search was beginning.

The next three days were the end times for small things, Cormac ruthless on his bloody path to destroy the divinity I had embodied. It was as if every rodent that had walked the earth lay massacred, the stone floors slick with foot falls of gore. Without regard Cormac leapt from windows onto the passing backs of great birds, downing seagulls and cormorants, impossibly by his jaws and weight. Sheep lay dead in the hills, throats peeled back like something had burrowed inside.

Even the monks were no longer safe as the cat stalked and tore at their legs, barely fending him off with kicks and brooms. Only Fionnlagh seemed immune to the cat's bloodlust; maddened with drink and a perverse love for his pet, he worked on his Gospel without cease, pausing only to drown the halls with ballads from his native Scotland, admiring the small carnages of his familiar as if they were desert miracles.

I found myself at an impasse, the moral implications of allowing Cormac to annihilate the transmogrified Christ unknown to me. My old self desired to lay low, to let the cat's carnage come to pass, hoping that my involvement would prove inconsequential or secret. But the self I had developed within me, the morality I had thought had permeated my body through the thoughts of my betters gave me courage. Trusting in his mentorship, I approached Fionnlagh in his chamber, where he sat doubled over his gospel, painstakingly illuminating a scene from Golgotha, Christ's body limp on the cross, his face a grimace of surprise and pain, an ink made from ochre providing the flesh a sickly pallor. Cormac lay asleep in his lap, muzzle mottled and red with rodent gore, enjoying a reprieve from his war path.

Before I could speak, I was met with Fionnlagh's sagging countenance, his eyes overly large and white, the pupils halved by lower lids. Cormac stared at me as the old abbott spoke, his voice stuttering and unnatural.

"It supposes communion Callum. It wishes to speak with you."

The sound of my own name shocked me, for I had not revealed it in all our time together, my birthright cast aside for the moniker of 'brother.' Cormac and the Abbot yawned in unison and the cat leapt to the floor where it stretched and sauntered to the cell door, looking back with a curl of its red lip, and I knew I was to follow. I looked at Fionnlagh for what would be the last time, and saw a man collapsing strangely, my friend's head and neck swaying at his navel like a pendulum.

The beast led me through the quiet stone of the abbey, the carved hallways and cobbles wet and dark from a dense mist that seeped in, robbing the abbey of its color and cheer. The monks had locked themselves away, remaining voiceless and hidden behind the wooden doors of their cells. And I felt as I do now, primed for a block, a rope. The abbey creaked and whistled, felt as if it was a living thing, the lungs of something great and heavy and still.

Cormac paraded me into the chapel, the light from outside battering its way in as thick heavy slabs, the windows dull arches of melancholic grey that rendered the jolly oaken pews and altar sodden and dour. At the foot of the altar there was a hole in the stone floor, a chthonic circle ringed with moss that had never been. The cat waited for me there, for my descent, the dark lariat of its tail swishing back and forth, the only sound in the world. Funny that I ever believed in salvation, that the things I had done could be washed away in the body and blood. That I could transmute into any terminal form, safe from the incursion of past and future selves.

I descended through the hole and into the fathomless catacombs beneath the abbey, where I crawled serpent-like through outer darkness. Cormac followed, and I could sense, it's true, bear- like bulk, it's demonic frustration that bubbled over into attacks on my bare feet, rending that soft flesh into ribbons and removing my smallest toe. I cried there in the darkness, shuffling past the corpses of interred abbots and kings, pushed on by the devil that was gnawing at my feet and yowling.

In the gloom I came upon a small cavern illuminated by cold, white light. I crawled to it, the frigid glow grew and built. I emerged into an oval cavity the size of an egg from which a grown man could hatch. And there, upon a bed of moss I saw the Christ, standing on its hindquarters, administering to a congregation of rodents, radiating the quavering brilliance of snow in the sun, its body mannered and gentle, pink and bald but for the curls of mannish hair that grew to its waist.

On hands and knees did I join the crowd of rodents, my head warmly surrounded by this furry flock that stood and gestured like men. Christ in his new form addressed us; he said, "Once there was a man who was cursed to be the same man. Always he went from place to place committing sin. And he was hungry each and every day, and evil and covetous each and every day. He was taken in by a farmer and his daughter."

WORLD'S LARGEST TURNIP

You are a turnip. One night a truck carrying experimental mutagens crashes into the field where you live. In the dead of darkness, the men in black come and sweep the wreckage away, disappearing everything without a trace as only they can. Deep in the soil you absorb the mutagens. The next morning you are twice as large as you were before. The next day four times. Things go on as such.

You become massive. Against your will, you starve all your turnip friends and become the only turnip in the field. Your farmer takes notice. He stands over you in bib overalls and says things like, "And how!" and, "Heee Doggy!" He quickly starts up an unrequited friendship with you. At night he visits you by lantern and eats his supper, speaking to you as if you are the reincarnated spirit of his dearly departed wife.

Things become strange, or stranger, between you and the farmer, and he becomes the big spoon. Regardless of how big you get he is always the big spoon. There was a time, when you were small, when you thought, in your primitive turnip way, that the farmer was God. Now that you are large, and the farmer cries into your crisp white flesh each night, you cannot account for these past thoughts. You are as big as the house. Barn swallows and robins peck nests into you and feed their young with your endlessly replicating flesh, giving you a chirping, swarming crown. You feel benevolent. On a warm dusk you take notice of the town, and the word "I" emerges from your mind.

The town takes notice back. People come from all over to see the World's Largest Turnip. The farmer charges 25 bucks a pop and makes a nice living. The men in black watch from the far side of the road, obscured in the fringes of a cornfield, speaking into their wrists and adjusting the malignant gleam of their sunglasses. Waiting.

Through your roots you begin to hear the Voice of the World. The Voice of the World expresses some misgivings about your growth, indicating that, if left unchecked, it might become a problem.

One day the farmer's son comes to him in tears. He tells the farmer that his dearly departed mother left him a note indicating that he is, in fact, the biological son of a car dealership magnate. He tells the farmer he is taking a paternity test, but will always think of the farmer as dad. The farmer is disillusioned but tries to make the best of it. He wants to meet the car dealership magnate.

They have coffee. Across from each other, they appear to be extremes of the same man, the unfortunate farmer residing on the less attractive end of the spectrum. The car dealership magnate roller skates, owns a house in Baja, California, and is effortlessly handsome in a way that implies generosity and ease. He is everything the farmer wishes he was made manifest.

The farmer continues to make the best of it although he is dying inside. He walks the fields at dusk and dawn staring daggers at you, as if the situation is all your fault. He stops making the best out of it. He starts carving symbols into the flesh of his forearms and yells aloud all the creative ways he is going to murder the call dealership magnate. He implies that your ultimate punishment will be to watch the long and creative murder happen. He is very, very confused about things.

On a golden October evening the farmer attempts to fornicate with you, using a paring knife to open a hole in your side. He fails multiple times and in multiple ways. You watch over his bumbling as a god, attuned to the world's gravity, the magnetic shield that prevents the sun from broiling all living things alive. You realize that if you continue to grow, you will, one day, be broiled alive. The Voice of the World wails for you to leave so nobody gets broiled. You have dreams of breaking away, of soaring through the cosmic weave, a turnip planetoid with its own gravitational field, a bird kingdom aloft in the reaches of space. You watch, with mild amusement, as the farmer's son witnesses the farmer's lewd behavior, as the farmer's son determines that he no longer views the farmer as dad.

Things get worse for the farmer. He goes unwashed and shuns human contact. He mumbles to heaven and earth. He haunts skinny dipping lovers, surprises hikers in the hills, becomes an urban legend. You start to feel worse and worse for the rapidly disintegrating farmer. You start to consider making him part of your escape plan, that perhaps your growing omniscience makes his happiness your responsibility. But every time the farmer comes back from the hills covered in feces and devouring a live fish, your sympathy resets, and you consider watching him broil.

After many months, Christmas comes around. The farmer, hiding from several arrest warrants, watches through a frosted window as his son mixes and mingles at the car dealership magnate's yuletide bash. He looks happier than ever, in a crisp green sweater, looking ever more like his replacement father. The farmer watches the car dealership magnate step out to count snowflakes, and before thinking too hard about it, opens the car dealership magnate's throat with his paring knife. He really loses it afterwards.

You are now a turnip that can be seen from space. You are making plans for your escape, for when shear mass tears you from the complaining ground and sends you on your cosmic voyage. The farmer returns from hiding in the hills covered in magnate blood. He proceeds to hack at your massive body with a wood chopping ax, truly believing that you are the reincarnated spirit of his unfaithful wife. This is your life for about a day and a half. You think really hard about the farmer dying until his eyes roll up and he does.

For three days his body goes unfound, administered to by the curious beaks of the robins and the sharp, hungry beaks of invading crows. He is found by his grieving son, who, having been aged by the loss of two dads, is now the spitting image of the departed car dealership magnate.

For three days you are left alone in your kingdom, the roadside visitors scared away by the farmer's downfall, interpreting you as a monument to his derangement. From your immense vantage point, you can see the curvature of the earth, the red lidded eye of the sun retreating from all life, fleeing so it seems. From your immense vantage point, you can hear the growing cries of doom and frustration erupting from the small inhabitants of the complaining world. You realize that it is time to get the hell out of dodge.

On a bright blue morning, you find yourself surrounded by vast concentric rings of men in black, their arrival instantaneous as only they can arrive. Their stillness disturbs you to your very core and you realize that you have not grown fast enough, that you never could have grown fast enough, that as large as you are and could be, the men in black would forever dwarf you.

You watch in terror as, from the curving horizon, the bright stars of surface-to-air-missiles launch and approach, the men in black heralding their arrival with a disconcerting, shambolic hum. In the moments of your impending destruction, you wonder as to why you were given such a life, such a vast, strange life. From your crown, nesting songbirds sing their loving reply, and you hope, that in death, your ashes sleep with theirs.

WHAT REMAINS OF THE GREAT ALCHEMIST (THE KNIGHT-PILE)

I am writing this down for posterity. So that I may not be confused with the guilty party if the worst should happen. I am not the great alchemist, but I am his nephew and apprentice, my duties mostly confined to the making of porridge.

The alchemist is currently locked outside, banging his fists bloody against the bolted door. It was me who locked him out there. In the great scheme of my life this is perhaps my greatest sin, though he is unwell with the sickness he created.

He is a charlatan, my uncle. I'm realizing that now as I go through his things. Much of what he called alchemy was simply the thoughtless combination of things he found in the forest or stole from castles. Anything expensive looking. He also may inadvertently be responsible for the end-times, if that messy pile of shambling knights is a sign of things to come. A fascinating thing to live next to, a snarling pile of snapping bones and squealing iron; flesh and armor and horse interlocked into a massive, bleeding lump the size of a small castle, undulating in the valley outside our tower where the pitched battle between the two great houses took place. All my uncle's doing of course. It was his love potion that helped one of the lords diddle the other lord's lady. It was that same lord who leapt from his horse onto the nearest pikeman and tore into his face, wrapping his limbs around the poor sod's torso. Then that pikeman bit another pikeman and wrapped him up, so on and so forth, till the battle became a knot of strange death. I do wonder what my uncle put in that potion. I've a note here that simply says, *'Lots of mushrooms. Some bones I found. Owl pellets. Powder, perfume, and place in something expensive looking.'* Lords, Ladies: my uncle the alchemist.

***

The pile appears to be eating itself—or trying to. It's been seven days and the pile seems to only grow, capturing at first the cautious squires who sought to loot or disentangle their mentors and then the scavenging wolves. Not to mention the single overeager bard who sought to commemorate the pile with his lute despite my bellowed warnings. He ventured too close and was dragged in by the ankles, a fate my uncle nearly suffered during his efforts to study the pile, instead suffering only a nip on the shin. Although perhaps his fate is more alarming. The blood of the pile is inside him. He screams at me from outside, alternating between insisting that he is fine and cursing my mother, which is doing him no favors. He bangs at the oaken door to the tower, rubbing himself against it. But I am no fool, nor do I have any interest in acquiring what he's got.

The night after his accident he ran feverish and wrong, moaning and laughing and gnashing his teeth against the cobbled floor of his study, shattering his teeth, contorting his limbs to their limits in a mix of rage and randy passion. He woke sedate the next morning with lidded eyes and slurred speech, a mere lull in preparation for his next fit. When next he left to study the pile, I refused to let him back in. Outside he will stay till this is sorted out, or until what courses through his veins sorts him instead.

***

I've reached a detente with my brain-addled uncle. I will occasionally throw loaves of bread down at him from the roof of the tower and he will cry a little bit softer at night. I've also agreed to be his proxy in developing a cure for the knight-pile, which is difficult as for most of the day and night he is a stark raving lunatic. In his brief hours of lucidity, he yells various ingredients at me, and I do my best to mix them together in his large cast iron chamber pot, ah, I mean alchemist pot. During his fits, I do my best to improvise. I use his various journals and recipe books, all of which, comprised of nonsense. For instance, one book is filled entirely with the names of what I presume to be whores. At first, I thought the names might be some sort of code; that was before I discovered the two Berthas, one qualified as 'Big Breasted.' Lords, Ladies: my uncle the alchemist.

So far none of our concoctions have proved successful. Most of what we throw into the pile produces only mild sizzling and is met by the excited, blood-curdling shrieks of the undead who seem to enjoy it. The most promising solution we have discovered so far is fire, although our dwindling supply of pitch restricts us to small, localized bonfires rather than the cleansing inferno that is required. I've sent word by owl to the surrounding kingdoms to send trebuchets. To send swords and spears. To send anything to remove this monstrosity from my front door. I mean my uncle's front door. No. I mean mine.

***

After some consideration I've started to eat the owls. Their constant hooting is making it hard for me to focus on my recreational dissections, a passion I may indulge in full now that my uncle is no longer here to disapprove. Well, he is still here, but outside. Screaming. He does that a lot now.

It seems that my uncle's perception of me was more nuanced than I realized. I long thought him to be a simple fool, which he is, but it seems that he has long held some deep-seated discomfort with me. After turning the aviary into my makeshift butchery, I took the liberty of going through his correspondences, where I discovered a series of letters between him and my father. I had assumed that they no longer spoke after my decision to leave home. It was a messy affair. The first and only time I ever saw my father weep. That poor violent man. I wonder if he's dead now. A tough bastard he was, possessing a certain brute genius as a blacksmith. But his dim mind provided him no outlet to his endless frustrations, asides from his fists, asides from his ruddy drunk's face. He hated my experiments. My ambitions. Every time I put a sick animal out of its misery, every time I searched its body for the source of its ills he'd fly into a rage, face turning red then purple. He was a stutterer, and his anger worked against him, robbing him of his words till he spoke them to me through my ribs. But he wept when I left, when my knave, purple-robed uncle sauntered into town, gold singing in his pocket, bright red alchemist's ring glittering on his little finger. How I coveted that ring! I always thought it strange that my father did not try to stop me. I was all he had.

These letters show me a different side of father. It seems he was a very sad man, that fatherhood hung heavy from his bones.

***

My uncle's condition has deteriorated. He has taken to circling the pile at night, body hunched and coiled, fingers splayed to the point of breakage, his silver hair swept across

92

his shoulders in a rangy mane. In a mere three days his body has vomited itself to gauntness and bone, his purple alchemist robes puddling around him as he stalks the valley, eyes black and bleeding, running like broken yolks. The image is nothing compared to the sound, the throaty cackling that escapes his liquified chest.

I met a shipwrecked man in a tavern once, who earned his drink on stories. He swore he'd been to a land where hermaphrodite dogs laughed in the darkness, eyes gleaming with firelight. They grinned he said, his eyes far away, they laughed and grinned like men. Then he imitated the sound and a certain tautness snapped in my mind. Something I'd felt loosen the first time I heard my father's knuckle crack against my jaw. It's hard to explain, but it felt like a rush of darkness, of mystery beyond the common brightness that surrounds us. What scarred that sailor, what had broken him, excited me.

I wonder where I'd be if I'd stayed with my father, instead of throwing in my lot with his knave brother, capable of little more than producing a copper from a child's ear. Would I be a blacksmith? Would I be a grave-robber? I suppose I could have been a doctor given my penchant for anatomy. But I was young and seduced by the glamour of it all. The iron into gold. The promise of miracles. That glittering red ring. The dark, laughing dogs.

I suppose he is something of an Alchemist after all. He's managed to transform himself and half the kingdom into a monster. The pile is growing larger, fed by a steady diet of crows and cutpurses fooled by the promise of an easy bite or pilfered coin. And yes, I suppose I could be more helpful. I could warn the poor souls that the knight-pile has learned to lunge, to tumble its mass of screaming gore in the direction of its choice. I could. But I don't. It's all very interesting to watch. A dark miracle as great and majestic as any mountain in God's spine. Dead knotted so tightly as to be a single thing, crawling with fires that texture the writhing mass in shadow.

Marvelous.

I do wonder what it is that my deranged uncle plans to do? He seems to be testing the pile, darting in and out of its range. Challenging it for dominance. Heaven above I hope he gets too close. It would be comforting to see him die this way, for once keeping the promises he sold to me: wonders outside of the dull mundanity of being a blacksmith's boy.

Soon it will all come to a head. Trees shake in the distance, swaying under the thunder of a thousand hooves. The king's army approaches. The great alchemist hears it too; he coughs his dog's laugh and scents the wind.

***

The king's army is a magnificent thing, a wall of gleaming riders bestride snorting chargers draped in color. Trebuchets and scorpions emerge from the treeline like massive beasts, fanged and cruel. I count more than a hundred flags in the line, houses unified in the extermination of the knight-pile, every man and boy who can swing a sword. I wonder if my father is down there, if he is still able-bodied enough to fight, if he's watching me now from the midst of this vast, brutal assembly.

I have a great vantage from the top of the tower, the scene unfolding before me as if set for my amusement. I have taken the liberty of wearing my uncle's purple robes, of borrowing his foppish hat and drinking from his jeweled chalice. If only I could recover his ring. The king's army believes me to be the great alchemist, and I suppose I'll do nothing to dissuade them. I wave. They raise their swords to me in salute. Fools. I see how my uncle so easily lived off their backs.

Speaking of my uncle, all remnants of his former, and

might I add, false, dignity has deserted him. He is now wholly an animal. A slavering, raving Grendel, visage marred by the rivulets of black blood that weep from his eyes and nose and mouth.

He stands between the king's army and the undead hillock, gesticulating at the gathered forces like a crazed ambassador for the dead, cackling between gouts of vomited ooze. For a moment all is silent, excepting the creaking armor and gasps that escape the knight-pile as it slumbers, near-dormant under the eye of the sun. Then an arrow embeds itself in my uncle's face, crunching through the tip of his nose. The force snaps his head back, neck splintering with a crack, but he does not fall. He stands, lolling, crudely gyrating and thrusting his hips towards the king's army, destroyed neck rolling his head along the back of his shoulders.

The next arrow finds his groin, the next seven his chest and guts, and I watch his pincushion corpse explode under a sea of charging hooves.

***

Well, this is a disaster. My uncle has, of course, once again found a way to ruin everything for everybody. I don't think I'll ever be able to unsee the image of his ruddy, burst corpse tearing off the top of the king's skull, clawed fingers buried deep within the orbital cavity, making jelly of the eyes. My God. He just wrenched the top right off, crown and everything, leaving just a brain and bearded jaw peeking out from a tottering suit of armor. I've flayed and dismembered my share of cats and dogs, but that was too much. After, the battle lost all appeal. If you could call it a battle. More of a strange consumption. After the amorphous-remnant-of-my-uncle half-decapitated the king, he went about creating his own undead pile, his wet, skinned-self at the tight center of it. The two piles then proceeded to crawl over each other, like slugs fornicating, the still living squealing and exploding into geysers of lumpy gore as the tidal forces of limbs and steel crushed them into pulp. Well at least it wasn't boring.

Now my tower watches over a singular, massive, writhing plateau made from the fusion of every able-bodied man in the kingdom. There is no valley anymore, just a bedrock of the dead, screams and cackles muffled by density, tight enough to walk over, maybe even to build on. Perhaps I'll start my own little kingdom. Why not?

***

I've finished reading my father's correspondences. It seems I was the reason he led such a sad life. It seems I was widely thought of as a terror, that the villagers did not appreciate my interest in their cats and dogs. It seems that my father thought me deranged, thought that my uncle's pseudoscience might be an appropriate outlet for my proclivities. I did not leave. I was let go. Interesting. I'm sure he's dead. I know it. And I don't think he's in the pile. I think he died in his forge, drowning in his tears. Perhaps I am sad about this. Perhaps not. I've never been quite able to tell.

***

I've eaten all the owls in the tower. All except one, should I need to contact the outside world. What's left of it that is. I feed him the remains of my experiments, my pickled cats and dogs and mice and frogs. The one unborn fetus I kept hidden at the bottom of my medicine chest, a rarity procured from the village headsman in exchange for an immortality brew of my own design. He was in the ground a week later. Dumb sod.

The world possesses a depth of silence I'd not thought

possible now that it has been emptied. In my mind's-eye I
see deserted castle hallways and market squares, dead leaves
touched by the chilling fingers of autumn wind, the occasional
whimper of a widow or orphan echoing from some deep
recess, a queen weeping across a vacant throne. It is a beautiful
silence, somehow deepened by the whispers of the glacial
dead that swallow my spire. I hear my father's words, words I
never heard him speak. They rise up from the letters of his last
correspondence, misspelled in his idiot's script, *'Brother. Beware
my son. Watch him. He is a dark hearted little boy.'* Dark hearted?
Dark hearted. Yes, I suppose. If this is evil, I can't say I'm not
intrigued.

I walk up and down the spire in my luxurious robes, my
purple silk, my foppish hat. The creak of the stairs, the groan
of the stone, the titters of the knight-pile feel like sounds in
my body: pops within my bones, blood rushing through my
veins. It feels as if I have expanded to fill this space and now it
is all me. I am the pile, and the pile is me. It's my creation. My
inheritance. Sure, my uncle's carelessness started things off, but
had I not tainted his porridge with the undead blood he would
never have become such a wonderful catalyst. Whoops. Did
I lie about that before? What did I write down? Something
about a bite or something? No matter. I no longer have need
to fear posterity. I poisoned him. I altered him. I put him into
my alchemist's pot and watched the recipe unfold. Why? I don't
know. I always thought about murdering him. It seemed like an
interesting thing to do. And look how it escalated things!

Perhaps this is not so bad of a situation. For me that is. It
seems pretty bad for everyone else. History is mine now. Not
exactly how I planned my ascendance, but alchemy is an inexact
science and everything and everyone is an ingredient.

From the roof of the tower, I watch over the knight-pile,
packed and near still, sleepy in its recent expansion. Yes, solid
enough to walk on, I reckon. I hope.

What remains of the great alchemist catches my attention, an arm protruding in search of moonlight, red sigil ring gleaming darkly, ready to be pruned like a rose. I know what I'll do. It's not the ring I need. It's the finger.

***

This shall be my last scribbling for a while, perhaps ever. If I survive, perhaps I'll burn this record, save it for comfort on a dark winter's night, when the chilled wind carries the dim corpse chatter through the windows of my tower, the dark stone where I, the great necromancer, rule on the back of an undead tide.

The last owl is fed and ready to embark upon its plague flight, my message to the village tied to its leg and digesting within its belly: my uncle's virulent finger.

They will send me sacrifices. They will send me more owls. I must say I have developed a taste for them. They will see what it is that I can spread, what I can send their way should I be displeased. It doesn't matter if the threat is false. If the pile is stagnant and dull. People have no end to energy when it comes to feeding monsters. I'll tell them the truth. Even if it's a lie. The knight-pile is hungry, and that is a certainty.

I watch as the confused bird takes flight, a dark nimbus receding into a bruised dusk, its flight already wobbly and of ill rhythm, my plague spreading through its body. One day all will be the knight-pile, bodies to cover every inch of this world. I'll be waiting here in my tower, waiting for what bubbles forth. Me, a dark hearted blacksmith's boy.

STARRY EYED OPHELIA AND THE SPACEMAN

The spaceman is a long and confusing black shape, rubbery and clumsy, a probing curiosity that visits me every dusk when the sun goes down, and the other creatures flee the sharks. He shines a bright light into my eyes. He tries to touch my brooding eggs. He extends a limp hand and waits for me to wrap a tentacle around an equally limp finger.

The spaceman circles around me, the falling sun red and burning in his strange glass eye, glamouring the bleached coral and pearlescent scallop shells of my nest pink. Sometimes the spaceman points a black box in my direction for purposes unknown, far be it from me to understand the glory of the spaceman. Perhaps it is a threat, a warning that I better start accepting that limp finger of communion. Perhaps the spaceman wishes to ravish me and I am rejecting said ravishment. My goodness!

When the darkness comes, when the sun sinks beneath the waves, the spaceman returns to his spaceship, a dark curvature floating high above. I am left alone with my future children, my little octopi who will slither out into the world and forget me. Who will eat my decaying body when I start to fall apart? The other octopi from my generation have already started disintegrating, shedding tentacles and skin as they tussle and limp around our brooding-ground, their lifespans dwindling. I could use a good ravishing before I dwindle. Perhaps if I brooded again, I could live again. Perhaps the spaceman will take me far away.

***

I always knew there was life up there amongst the stars, separate from the water which is all I know there to be. The other octopi think I'm crazy, think my obsession with the spaceman is wrong and unnatural. They do not understand. They are not beloved like me. They do not understand that it is not an obsession but a courtship, that if he asks, I will attempt to give him beautiful spaceman babies. The other octopi ask me how I know the spaceman is from space.

They say, "Ophelia, have you ever seen his spaceship rise from the water and fly up, up and away? Because we sure haven't." I tell them I do not need to. I tell them I have faith.

Oscar the Cuttlefish shares my belief in the spaceman, although I think there is nothing that Oscar does not believe in. He says he was once abducted by the space people and experimented on in a place called Effervescent Gardens. He says the reason he covers his tentacles with scavenged tinfoil is to prevent the space people from reading his thoughts. He says he wants nothing to do with the spaceman and neither should I. Oscar is not supposed to be here, he is supposed to be with the Cuttlefish. He says that is the first place that the space people would look. He says he is hiding in plain sight.

***

The spaceman comes to visit me, and I accept his finger. I wrap a tentacle gently around it and crawl my way along the spaceman's body, allowing him to twirl us around the soft, glowing waters. We dance across the reef, the hungry barracudas shimmering in the hazy distance, the looming shadows of sharks unsubstantial in the glow of our entwined hearts. I always knew I was meant for more romantic things than brooding, for waiting out my flesh in a nest of bones with the rest of the idiots. My spaceman will take me away and make me a cosmic bride and we'll live in a castle made from starlight filled with half-breed children who never gestate.

The spaceman returns me to my nest and struggles to remove me from his embrace, prying my tentacles away one at a time. Coquettish, I refuse to yield. I do not want our dance to end. His breathing grows deep with excitement, flailing his body, unable to control his arousal at my forwardness. He uses both hands to throw me away, tearing my smallest tentacle slightly. So chaste! The sun departs leaving our reef in gloom. He floats just beyond me, recedes into dimness, dark rubbery skin fusing with the velvety surface of the sea and the dark stellar beyond.

When he is gone, I puddle into my nest and swoon. Oscar watches me from the dark edge of the reef, where the coral falls in a sheer drop into the fathomless beyond. He flashes colors across his body: blues, greens, and reds spilling and curling around each other in hypnotic patternless patterns. Not entirely bad to look at, that Oscar. I wonder if he is suicidal in addition to being crazy, watching me out in the open like that, surrounded by hungry mouths, moonlight glinting off his tinfoil. He probably just loves me. They all love me. Brave knight, know that I am promised to another. Sigh.

***

Oscar has reluctantly agreed to be my go-between as long as he does not have to be physically present during any torrid rendezvous. He warns me to reconsider any association with the spaceman. Jealous Oscar. He says the spaceman will expect something on the third date.

Oscar's knowledge of the space people is overheard and incomplete, built upon his sleuthing in captivity, but he believes that whatever happens on our third date will make the spaceman very, very happy. He suggests I feel the situation out. when I ask him to clarify, he changes colors very quickly and scoots away which clarifies nothing.

***

The spaceman has brought a spacewoman into the mix and, suffice to say, I am a little upset. Perhaps he is just nervous, perhaps he needs her to confirm for him that I am indeed receptive to his charms. I'm sure there is nothing to worry about. She mostly just holds the blackbox while the spaceman and I dance.

***

I am unsure of how to progress things. Our third date came and went like all the others, pleasant enough, but with no change to our romantic routine. Honestly our dancing is starting to get stale, the reef less and less magical with each twirling go-around. When will he take me to his great beyond? I don't have long before I too start to disintegrate. The males are already dying en masse. Losing tentacle after tentacle, spiraling into the shallows or the depths till something hungry makes a meal of them. Oh, poor boys of my youth, the anonymous father of my brood still out there among you, dead or dying.

My young squirm beneath me, I can see them coiling their little tentacles through the yellow, glowing translucence of my eggs. Children, I've sworn Oscar to your protection should I be spirited away. If anything, he shows more interest in you than I ever have, watching over me as I sleep, watching over you. Shameful as it is, I have often viewed you as a simple side effect of my life. A thing that would have happened regardless of my choices. I would have woken up with you one day, my slithering brood, as sure as death. You'll be little monsters regardless of who's here to watch you become. Try not to eat Oscar little ones, he is a simple soul.

***

The blackbox is a thing called a camera, a magic device that the space people use to own and manipulate reality, to hold things as they are so they don't become what they will be. The spaceman is using his camera to make me a star, to keep me from growing into death with the rest of my generation. Yet, I feel ill every day. Oscar begs me to stop, to go away with him, to swim into the deep blue, just the two of us, before the spaceman sucks me dry. He says what good is posterity if it kills my present. Poor Oscar, he doesn't know, he's never been in love. I give of myself freely to the spaceman, so that he can gorge himself on my life while we're apart and leave me none of it. He captures me for me, and devours for the both of us. Silly Oscar, he must be tired of being wrong all the time, must be sad that he is dying too.

***

The spaceman is coming to break my heart. I feel it. I have felt it coming for some time.

Since the spacewoman arrived, our dances have gone stale.

He is swimming towards me and already there is something different. Gone is his black rubber skin, replaced by pale and wimpy flesh. Perhaps he is molting? Perhaps this new unsightly softness will harden into the dusky firmness I was once so smitten by?

His shedding has revealed a new appendage, one even limper than his finger, growing from between what Oscar calls legs, two wrinkly sacks hanging beneath it.

The spacewoman follows behind him, grasping him as they descend as one. Her body is different, lacking that central tentacle, but owning two massive swells that the spaceman cannot keep his hands off.

They circle around me and glow, gold and crimson light caressing their pale bodies as the sun sets. Am I to be part of this? They start to entwine. Am I to join? The spaceman's limpid finger becomes un-limpid, joins with the spacewoman in the place where she does not have one. I guess I'll try, how bad can it be? Perhaps this is how space people take wives. Anything to get away from here. From my children. From my decaying body.

The spaceman places his camera on the coral boulder where the clownfish live. He turns the spacewoman around to look into it, thrusting into her curved backside. My word! I know brooding when I see it. I will not be left alone. I will not be denied my stars. Not after giving so much.

I grasp the spaceman's ankle and coil around his leg, pulling upwards and squeezing his sacks to show I mean business. The spaceman screams, the sound ugly and tremulous in the salty water. He struggles to look, removing his tentacle from the space woman, who also screams, and starts laughing. She points the camera at me as I squirm, as I do my best to please the spaceman as she does. But my love, he is struggling, squeezing and tearing my delicate body. Was it all just a game? Is what he has stored away from me enough to discount my future? Am I not to be protected to the end as the world grows dark?

I feel pieces of myself break, see my tentacles spiral away from me, my blue blood clouding the glowing pink water, small fish emerging from the coral to feast on my remains. I feel them all over. I am being eaten alive.

Broken, I float down to my nest reaching out for a final chance. The stars, the stars. The stars wait for me. I find the spaceman's tentacle, limp again, and squeeze. He really loses it then, thrashes and squeals, his cries muffled and dense in the vibrating brine. The spacewoman laughs harder, chest orbs undulating in rhythm to her merriment.

I am pulled upward. I am ascending towards the surface, to the sky beyond. Riding the spaceman to his waiting spaceship, his spacewoman next to us, trying to remove me from the tentacle, not finding my involvement funny anymore.

As we rise the sun dips below the curve of the sea. A great green flash erupts, blinding us, igniting the reef with phosphorescent lambency. Through the quivering surface I can see a saucer hovering above the spaceman's humble craft, spinning with impossible light, the green beam pouring from its humming center. The spaceman is frozen, his limbs unmoving, jaw slack in disbelief, and yet we rise still, the three of us borne upwards, weightless in the green shining. I should've known. He is no spaceman; he is as earthbound as I am. But unlike him, I am not afraid. The true space people have arrived.

As we break from the water, I give the reef one final look, the spread of peaked coral spectral and beautiful in the saucer's strange glow, close to the castle of light from my dreams. Oscar watches me, his tin foil glinting green. But of course, it's not tinfoil. It's armor. Oh, brave knight I will never forget you.

Outside the water the man and woman's screams turn shrill and harsh, unpleasant to say the least. They do not deserve the space people as I do. The man and woman cling to each other, squishing me between them. Free of the ocean their jerky motions are violent, damaging me further. I can't breathe. My body becomes heavy and brutal, the ocean pulling me back, stretching me apart.

The bright center of the saucer is so close, the green light destroying my vision with its brilliance. I am nearly blind. Blood is draining from my body. Dripping down and pattering on the surface. I never considered the possibility that I wouldn't make it.

"Take me with you!" I scream with the colors of my body, "Take me with you!"

But they won't. I am melting on the cold floor of the spacecraft. The man and woman huddle nearby as strange chattering voices echo around us. Grey, hunched forms lurk in the dimness, blurry to my singed eyes. The man and woman scream, animal and deep, my conceptions of them unmade in the depravity of their sound. I beg the space-people for mercy, as I am nudged away, nudged and nudged until I am falling, falling back to sea. And overhead, the great saucer spins into a horizon line of light and departs forever with my dreams.

***

Oscar finds me in the shallows, carries me gently back to my nest, my pile of bones and shells, my unfeeling brood that will never love me as a mother, although I guess I never gave them the chance. He sings to me as I die, his armor crumpling against my flesh, a crinkling language of the heart. He is missing tentacles too. He too is falling apart.

"They almost got you," his skin says, "they almost got you."

"Oh, silly Oscar," my skin says back, "Always looking for love in all the wrong places."

SWITCHBACK JACK 3: HOMECOMING

Glass. Beer. Repeat. Don't get cheap on me. Not here on the final lap. My son's thirty-one now. Which meant Switchback Jack came for him one more time back when he turned twenty-four. I'm not going to lie; it just wasn't the same without Leary. I don't think I ever gave him enough credit for what he brought to the table. If anything, he's Jackson's true godfather, not Joan's do-nothing younger brother who died when the towers went down. But that's neither here nor there. Point is I had to step up in a way I'd never had to before to finish my son's education. And part of that meant fabricating a terminal illness, losing three-fourths of my body mass, and faking my own death. We'll get there. Don't look at my stomach. Don't you ever fucking look at my stomach. For now, let's start with the renovations.

Given my son's maturity during this third go around, I thought trying for a sort of psychological-horror situation might be the best course of action. Instead of terrifying Jackson instinctually, I wanted to terrify him existentially. So, a year after killing his friends, excuse me, after all his friends were killed by circumstances beyond my control, I had the contractor behind Universal Studios Haunted Halloween Nights hollow out the walls of the Vermont house so that a grown man of about my height could scamper between the floors and appear anywhere at any time. I'm not going to get into the details here, but imagine ropes, rungs, hatches, trick doors, two-way mirrors, tubular slides and you'll get the idea.

The next and most important step was creating the atmosphere. And by that, I mean haunting the living shit out of this town. Now this took time, so I started the process right after the funerals to give myself the full eight years. First off was devaluing the place and getting rid of the skiers and tourists, something accomplished easily enough with a few dead drifters showing up around the mountain, eyes gouged and pulverized with branches, roots sewn into their guts, teeth removed and replaced with acorns. Trick is to pay other drifters to do the dirty work. Let me tell you, much of America has been built on this very principal, drifters hired to kill other drifters. After that it was a matter of waiting out the failing businesses, the renters, the homeowners, evicting a bit here, foreclosing a bit there. I had some fingers in the local banks, it always helps to have some fingers in the local banks. I have some fingers in a bank in Aruba where I'm not dead. Point is, ruining a town is a bit like making a long putt, you have to know the cut of the green and all you've got to do is tap and watch the ball roll in. After a couple of years, I didn't even have to hire drifters anymore, they just came on their own! The loose limbed, feral-eyed highwaymen of America, loping through empty streets like half-changed werewolves. Of course, I couldn't give them the run of the place. Haunted places need to have some sane residents to acknowledge the place as being such. So, I had the drifters cull themselves occasionally and kept the important places open: general stores, bait and tackles, the local brewery, which might I add makes a fine amber ale. Cheers, and yes another.

I found the brewery to be the best investment, towns with

a large single source of employment seem to be a bit haunted to begin with. And the booze helped with the drunks. Ah yes, my beautiful, beautiful drunks. That was my masterstroke. You see, knife-fighting drifters are terrifying, sure, but what a haunted town really needs, what it strives for, is a perpetual reminding machine, a storytelling apparatus to maintain the legend of why things are as terrible as they are. So, I put drunks on retainer, paid them to take method acting and hired voice coaches to get them to sound like Captain Quinn from Jaws. Once a year I subjected this stable of drunks to torturous hypnotic suggestion in a secret, concrete bunker the C.I.A wasn't really using, layering their minds with free associative imagery of root-gouged eyes and night vision stills of Tom Leary murdering teenagers. Let me tell you, dozens of brainwashed drunks in a government black-site. It's a sight to behold, some real slapstick. Mix in a few drifters well… Anyway, a finished drunk was a drunk who truly believed Switchback Jack haunted the mountain and skulked the trails, disemboweling at will, replacing the organs of murder victims with dead squirrels and other woodland debris. A perfect drunk was one that wholly believed the latter and pulled off Captain Quinn with gusto. Only churned out one of those beauties.

So that was the set-up, the production if you will. Next came the hard part—the dying part. The saying goodbye part, which was fake but needed all the emotional trauma of being real. For Jackson's benefit, of course. My own dad died of cancer, so I knew what to do for the most part, how to waste away cinematically and bring everyone down with me.

Jackson was back with his mother after graduating from college, frustratingly listless given all I had done for him, back to selling drugs to high school seniors. But he had the tools, I could see that, an apathy that bordered on cruelty, a willingness to remove a toenail from the poor and rich alike, whoever came up short. When it came to commerce Jackson was not very interested in credit. Good boy. Did I tell you he works in government?

So, he had the right kind of sociopathy to do big things in the world, but he was also sad and mopey, a little bit boring even. For whatever reason he was convinced the world did not have good things in store for him. Which, ugh! Young people am I right? Of course, you wouldn't understand. You probably have residual memories of the birth canal.

Our relationship was pleasant enough, when I was allowed to see him that is. I patted him on the back and asked him about his dreams, if there was anyone special in his life, not many since the whole cheerleader decapitation. We watched football and drank by the six pack, but there was, how shall I put this, a hollowness to him, something inside that needed to be jump-started. What he needed was motivation, that same perpetuating legacy I gave the town. And so I went about haunting him. Mind you, nothing motivates a child more than being haunted by unresolved issues with their parents. If you want them to be successful, it's the single greatest gift you can give them. Now I can't imagine Jackson had many problems with my parenting, but he did have issues with Switchback Jack, so the idea was to funnel that trauma, helpful trauma mind you, into my death, linking the two forever and ever and ever.

And so, I ate a fistful of tapeworm eggs and went about emaciating myself. I drank thimbles of blood, egg-whites, and raw veal on the sly and hacked them up as simulated lung slop. I did this for months, even when Jackson wasn't around, burrowing into the idea of being terminal with my totality. At night I wandered the house buck-naked muttering under my breath, wheezing and rubbing my member against the crystalline cold of the windows, searching the shifting gloom for the unmistakable lope of the Wendigo. I pretended that I too was haunted, an illness within and without. I told myself I saw strange, gnarled tree people standing at the dark fringes of the wood. And I did see strange, gnarled tree people at the dark fringes of the wood. They entered the house and stood above me while I pretended to fitfully sleep, their bodies cracking at the joints with each splintering twist.

Now this wasn't fun per se, I mean have you ever had more than one tapeworm inside you? Let me tell you, they fight, they compete. They exit your mouth when you're eating cereal and drink the milk from your bowl. But sacrifice is required when entering a story. If I've learned anything from dear sweet Leary, it's the value of pretending, how easily the pencil line between reality and fiction is rubbed away.

Now, in case you're wondering how I got away with faking stage four pancreatic and stage three lung, being friendless and divorced was the silver bullet. Without anyone else on hand to counter my narrative, Jackson was alone as the counterpoint to my schtick. And it wasn't like Jackson at twenty-four had any understanding of oncology. What he thought was chemo was me getting nutrients dripped into my body so that the tapeworms wouldn't kill me. In his eyes I was just his creepy, dying father. He called me that when I listened in on his phone calls. In a way I remember those days fondly. They represent my last real quality time with my son, the two of us riding in silence to and from my fake treatments, his face dark and sphinx-like, stoic but for the quiver in his hands, still a little chicken shit.

My last wish was for Jackson to spend a final weekend with me back at the Vermont house. He wasn't too keen on the idea, but his mother straightened him out with some grade-A guilt tripping. I think Jackson's insistence on drug peddling wore away at her on some moral level. She was more than happy to shrug him off to me during those last few months. I know the feeling. The week before my dad died, he thought all the hammered nails in our house were crawling insects. We had our differences, but Joan's a good woman. She's since remarried a golfer on the amateur circuit. Sometimes I watch them from the dark fringes of the woods. But that's not really part of the story.

Anyway, Jackson and I packed bags and made our way up north, to Switchback, to the mountain, to the house. Jackson hadn't been back since Leary beat him half to death with his girlfriend's noggin. Which I guess I can understand.

It was the two of us plus my nurse, Janet, who of course wasn't really a nurse but rather a very skilled and very well paid practical FX artist from Weta. Peter Jackson's a good friend of mine. If you ever get him on your podcast, tell him I said hi. Tell him that I watch him from the dark fringes of the woods, that he looks good without all the weight.

What can I say about Janet? Maestro. Genius. Confident. All of these things? Maybe none. Turns out hosting such a large number of parasites can wear you down quite a bit. By the time Jackson got me up to the house I was blacking out pretty frequently. I'm not even sure what happened to her, if she ever got out of the walls. Anyway, I at least know she did her job with a baseline degree of competency seeing as the whole enterprise worked. Well, until it didn't. Her chief jobs were to shoot me up with adrenaline every night so that I could scamper around inside the walls, and to dress my body and sheets every morning to make it look like I was shedding bloody sap and pine needles, the idea being that I was transforming into Switchback Jack. And I think it worked, although I may have started to shed actual parts of my insides as well, seeing as how my stomach was painfully distended with worms. I SAID DON'T LOOK AT IT! But I vividly recall doing things like clawing Jackson's face through the false back of a vanity mirror and dangling from a rustic chandelier like a feral spider monkey. I couldn't have done any of those things without being hopped up on horse serum.

All said and done the whole haunting was a great success,

despite the times Jackson caught me and wrestled me back into bed and wouldn't let me do any haunting. Yes, I slipped up. Despite all my preparation, I was on the wrong side of sixty and many months pregnant with tapeworms. In all my planning I'd never considered the fact that, perhaps, I was not physically capable of shimmying through crawl spaces and pushing through revolving bookcases. So yes, there were a few times when Jackson had to knock through the wall with a fire poker to prevent me from asphyxiating in a folded clam position. But aside from that, I think he was really fooled, really terrified and scared by the experience. He cried all the time. Little chicken shit. When no one was looking he called his mother and cried about how he hoped it would be over soon. Good boy. Soft boy. Chicken shit boy. I told you he's a senator, what I didn't tell you was that he's a Democrat.

The night I died I wanted some alone time with Jackson to say our goodbyes. So, I stripped naked, and lured Janet into a false-backed armoire, trapping her inside the walls. Let me tell you, stripping naked is a great tactic to get people to follow you, they pretty much have to, it's a social contract thing, especially if you're elderly and people suspect you of being soft in the head. While Jackson was busy trying to fire-poker Janet free, I emerged from a carpeted trapdoor and stuck him with a sleeping dose of morphine. I told you I got caught doing my schtick a few times, I didn't tell you I was bad at it.

It took Jackson a little bit to pass out, a lot of fumbling for the telephone and telling me he wished I was dead. It was probably the least chickenshit thing he'd ever said to me. He conked eventually and I brought him to his bed for our tear-jerking scene. I watched him sleep, the same way I did when he was a baby and I was terrified he'd die spontaneously. Children are beautiful. They really are. We bring so much terror into each other's lives. It's beautiful. I fastened my Switchback Jack mask to his face with sap and hot glue, as a final lesson, a token of my affection.

Having completed my son's education, I departed through the window, making sure the sheer curtains billowed behind me as I left. Outside the night was full moon perfect, the wind moving the forest with under-water smoothness. I pissed on a shrub and howled, naked and feral with my legend. I like to think that somewhere, out in the wild dark, barely safe within the primeval grip of firelight, somebody heard me and looked up.

Look, let's be real here for a second, maybe you think I'm a monster. That I'm crazy. That I drink too much and sound somewhat like Captain Quinn. You think I'm bad. Evil. And for what? For being radical? For parenting my child in the same fucking way the movies do? God knows they do most of the heavy lifting now. You tell me, if you've got kids, count the hours they spend with Michael Myers and compare it to the time they spend with you. Name one parent who's not interested in haunting their child, who doesn't want to stick around forever, past the grave and into the genealogy. You take little Tommy to Disneyland not because YOU enjoy it, but because they do, because one day that connection might be the only posthumous lifeline you get.

Sorry.... excuse me for a second. The tapeworms are acting up. Don't look at my stomach, please. It agitates me when people look at my stomach. Don't leave. I'm not done. You think I'm a bad dad. I'd like another drink. Just one. it's not because I'm desperate, it's so I can make you understand. I still see my son. We visit. He just doesn't know we visit. I watch him from the dark fringes of the woods, through the windows, as he grows. He's a senator. Didn't I tell you that? I'm not sure of what state. He's married to a woman who looks a lot like Janet, although I don't think that can be, seeing as how she's in the walls. Maybe he got her out. They have novelty wash towels. I stole one. They say 'Janet Jackson.' Isn't that funny?

Obviously, I didn't really die. I'm right here at the bar talking to you. And maybe you're thinking that I'm just a drifter. Perhaps, one of my own drifters. I'm not. I am THE drifter. I came from one life to another. Some men have another family on the side, me, I have iterations. I planned and executed the perfection of fatherhood. I made my son imaginative, and strong, and unfortunately just a little compassionate. But whatever. You can say many things of the life I gave him, what you can't say is that it was boring. And now, now, I'm Tom Leary, that's what the license says when it has to. And sometimes, when the moon lies low and murderous, and somebody's in the woods all alone, well, then I'm Switchback Jack. I've always been.

DISASSEMBLY

The Man loved the staircase. It was his favorite part of the house; a free-floating spiral structure with a cylindrical hanging light that spread his shadow around the walls. It made him look like an explosion. Sometimes he would stand there for hours and stare at this disassembly. Sometimes it was all he did.

He never felt like the house was haunted. After his reconstruction, when he was something new, he could not remember the events. He had either died or been born. Perhaps there was no difference; oblivion was left in his wake.

***

He woke up one night because of the cold. It ate through his bones under the sheets.

For a while he simply watched his breath materialize as wet exhaust. Then he got up and walked to the staircase. Standing there he radiated his arrangement of shadows. He moved his body like a marionette, observed how the dark reflections of himself jerked and swayed in response. He took notice of each and every piece. He could not decide which dictated which. His self or the image of himself. And there in the dewy cold night on the top of the stairs it began. He noticed something odd in his shadows, an intangible difference that puzzled him. The silhouette of his right arm was not where the light demanded it be. It was missing.

He checked that it was still part of his body. It was not. He felt the shoulder joint the arm had once called home. It was now a smooth lump of flesh with a nub of perfectly round bone underneath.

With his remaining arm he removed his shirt and stood there. Somehow the lack of the body part did not disturb him; he was in fact comforted by a sense of warmth that pervaded him and seemed to radiate outwards, heating the environment. He descended the stairs and entered the kitchen. With his one remaining arm he made himself a sandwich and stared at the wall of darkness outside the window. He noticed something floating in the window's glassy surface. His missing arm, perfectly represented in the black square where his own reflection should be. He had no words for it. He touched the window: it felt like a window. The arm remained preserved within the span of night. Then daylight came and obliterated it. He watched this happen, sitting on a stool in his white linoleum kitchen. He ate a sandwich that tasted like buttery joy.

***

The Man stopped going to his custodial job at the research laboratory. He started dabbling in arts and crafts at his own leisure. He became remarkably adept at using only his left arm. He found a rare talent in that neglected appendage that had always been hidden by the relentless tyranny of his dominant arm. With the dominant appendage removed from the equation he discovered his left arm had a rather devastating talent for art. With unfettered delight, it proceeded to fill canvases with wonderful swirls of yellow and blue oils, the end result being abstract fields of flowers underneath a green sky. He no longer felt gnawing existential hunger.

He no longer felt the need to compulsively masturbate. He attempted compulsive masturbation several times, but was thwarted by a stark refusal from his left arm. It simply refused to function normally in the event of masturbation, leaving his junk mashed and sore. It didn't matter: his junk was the next thing to go.

The next day, The Man woke up on the floor covered in blue morning light. His crotch was a smoothed spongy patch without the burden of greedy nerve endings. For several childlike moments he practiced punching himself.

***

He found the missing organ that night while cleaning out the pornographic material from his basement. It was his intention to burn such things. And so he did, rather absentmindedly, on the concrete floor of his cellar. And there he saw it. The frozen representation of his missing penis floating in the fire fueled reflection cast upon the cellar window, a wilted red thing that now looked like a pair of fleshy eyes and a long bulbous nose. The smell of burning porn bothered him enough to retreat from the basement. He no longer thought of his missing johnson. He felt wonderfully sexless.

***

In the coming days, The Man discovered wonderful new things about himself. His mind became a peaceful nest of sensitivity and empathy. For the first time he found himself truly capable of listening, and more importantly, caring about what people had to say. Especially women. He had never been able to fully speak or listen to women. In all instances something would distract him, born from the fact that he would at some point, in any conversation or exchange, think about reproducing. Without the burden of sexual thought, The Man found himself to be quite the ladies' man, or as much of a ladies' man as a one armed, de-johnsoned individual could be.

On several occasions he created deep and heartfelt relationships with such women. They of course viewed him as something completely asexual and non-threatening, which he eventually found to be okay. In fact, he felt pretty damn special knowing he was non-threatening. He felt it beat being a lot of other things in the world. He could have been a mass murderer: by chance he was not. And he still had the talents of his rapturous left arm that could show things to the minds and hearts of the world. Being able to show rapturous things to the hearts and minds of the world made him feel happy.

***

The Man's dopey sense of peace evaporated when he woke up one morning to find his beautiful arm removed from his torso. At first he met this development with extreme anger. He exploded through his house checking the windows for the stolen appendage. He foamed at the mouth and chewed bath towels. He found the missing appendage in the living room where it hung open-palm in the glass of a French window. He begged the French window to return the arm to him. With his teeth he dragged one of his lovely paintings to the living room and showed it to the window. He gesticulated wildly at the fantastic oil painting; he showed the window how he had swirled pink azaleas with his thumb, how he had created hazy summer distance with gentle love touches; he tried to explain three-point perspective; he tried to show how each moment of elegant precision given to him by his glorious arm was a pure extension of his soul. The window didn't really care. It did not appreciate the hazy summer distance. It did not understand three-point perspective.

In his rage, The Man did what any normal, armless individual would do. He accosted the expertly crafted French window with his head, butting repeatedly till his face was a ruin and the window was smeared with homeless blood. This did not move the thoughtless window to benevolent restitution. It did, however, knock The Man unconscious. When he woke, he no longer had a tongue.

***

It was at this juncture in The Man's disassembly that people began to take notice. After losing his arms and tongue, The Man cut a rather obvious figure, an obvious figure that lacked the communicative tools to explain away his situation. The throngs of intellectually romanced women would often find him cackling absent-mindedly outside his house, howling as if the residence itself had done him some great disservice. The Man was no longer wearing clothes.

The throngs of women collectively decided that, perhaps, The Man had donated parts of himself to science. Science was perhaps rather villainous in its acceptance of such valuable pieces. But it didn't really affect their well-being, so eventually the women forgot about The Man and stopped bringing him things like muffin baskets and self-validation. The Man became something of a pariah. He stopped being known by people, and thus stopped being a person.

It was hunger that eventually redeemed The Man from his cackling depression. Fueled by his need to feed, The Man found that his legs had become remarkably toned and athletic; his eyes had become sharper; his ears more deft and sensitive; his nose awoke to the hidden smells of the universe. With his awakened senses and newfound agility, The Man learned to stalk the woods near his home like a predator. At top speeds, he found he could outpace deer; he found he could leap upon their backs and bite their necks open; he found he could savagely consume their raw and grisly flesh; he found they tasted like copper and happiness.

And so, The Man stopped being a man. He became instead a wild hunter-beast that ruled a forest kingdom. He was not entirely devoid of his former self. At dusk and dawn, he often found himself in high-up places, marveling at the changing of the light. He saw in these moments the very beast-heart of Earth, Mother Gaia uncloaked in chthonic nudity; the sky progressing from the deepest blue to the softest gold through gradients of color imperceptible to the human eye.

How the sky itself had a smell, the cold and clean smell of pine and water. And in these hours of rest, he comprehended the most purely felt peace. The peace of green fir trees as they swayed in dawn's heartfelt breeze. He no longer experienced time like a human. He experienced time like an animal, and so he lived an eternity running through nature with the wind in his hair.

***

One sad day the Former-Man-Current-Beast woke without his legs. His humanity came crashing back. He found himself immobile save for his mouth and his torso which he could twitch. He was neither shocked, nor surprised: this was inevitable. He found that he was crying. He found that he was awash in thankful melancholy that he had the joy of the forest in his past. Then he went blind.

***

And so, the Once-Again-Man proceeded to wiggle and

mouth himself back to his home.

The passage was arduous. The roots and rocks of the forest floor clawed at his body, tearing horrible wounds in his soft needy flesh, as if the forest could not yield him back unwillingly. Yet he continued. The flesh was constantly stripped from his stomach till his ribs glistened in the ruddy mess that was his body. Yet he continued. When it became too much, he used his mouth. He pulled himself forward with great chomps of grass and dirt. It tasted beautiful. And he continued.

The journey took three days. After the first night he lost his ears. He could not hear the animals that came to witness his passage. They stood at a distance; their ancient minds possessed of a great sadness. None tried to eat him; none tried to help him. Not till the third and final day when his mouth closed up, did a lone wolf proceed to lick his wounds with a tenderness that made The Man cry. He did not have the eyes to show it, but his heart bawled with loving appreciation. And finally, when The Man somehow rolled his sightless, unfeeling body up the porch steps and into the door, the animals turned and retreated into their green depths. Thus did they worship their fallen king.

***

And so, The Man returned to the place that had claimed him. He did not have the faculties to see the fragments of his body which now littered each and every window of his home. But the pieces were suspended in timeless reflection: the notches of his spine lost amongst the kaleidoscopic twinkle of the chandelier, embedded in shadows like bone stars; his tongue lolling amidst amorphous wax in the halogen glow of a lava lamp; his teeth and fingernails visible in the soft corners and shine of plates and coffee mugs; his heart pumping dimly in the spiritless Plexiglas on his microwave; lost nerve endings erupting like lightning storms in the sectioned eyes of flies swarming around porch lights. He felt himself heaved and expanded; a man turned into a pulsing cloud.

***

For several days The Man waited to die. He was tremendously peaceful. He had a timeless sensation of floating. He did not realize that his torso was the last piece to depart, leaving only a nondescript ball of pink flesh at the top of the staircase where he once so vapidly stared at the nothingness within him. Now as a simple piece, he was so much purer than he had ever been before; a mind in a fleshy ball waiting for the thoughts to dim and die. Waiting for the light that he himself created to be expunged by the foreword tread of cosmic information. He could not see what it was that happened around him. How the pieces in the windows somehow materialized and reformed into a headless body that sought him for days on end. Staggering around the house in unseeing desperation until the day its familiar hands wrapped around him and placed him upon its neck. From his rightful perch, The Man saw the world regrow around him. His eyes and mouth emerged from the flesh with a gentle puckering sound. He could again hear the wind. He could again taste the air. And so he was made whole. There remained, though, a certain sensation of disembodiment, as if he was no longer in control of the ship; as if he existed mostly in a single piece of himself, a certain arm he had developed affection for.

***

The Man found himself out on the grass watching his house burn. From the window his shadow stood watching. It waved to him once and then it too burned.

***

He went on to a life without memory. He existed in pieces and moments. One day he died and some people said some things about him.

THAT RAMBLING, SHAMBLING
PASSWORD MAN

It creeps into existence through the splitting monitor,
pulling itself free with twisted hands of Cambria, Helvetica
and Times New Roman, a body of black text writhing like
font centipedes, flashes of compressed video pulsing deep
inside. It lies there, fetal and confused, a pile of echoes, tirades
and archival memory. It takes a few tries to work the legs
right, rising on wobbling knees till, eventually, it stands like
Brody. Walks like Brody. Descends the staircase with the same
shambling thunk. But it's not Brody, just a mad buzzing ghost
made up from the pieces he left behind.

Genny's asleep on the couch with the television on. The
first deep sleep she's had since Brody died. She's kept the
pictures on the mantel without knowing why, the misleading
photographs of two happy people with arms around each
other, no evidence of the bruises on her thighs, the purple rings
around her neck.

You can imagine her surprise when she wakes and finds
Brody 2.0 sitting in Brody's familiar chair, shoulders sloped
with the same simian aggression, hand cupped for a whiskey-
cola that isn't there, that won't be coming.

"A-nnnn-no-therrrrr," the Brody shape manages through a garble of dial-up, miming a final gulp, face sliding every which-way in a jigsaw of social media tirades. Video flickers inside his brow, a MPEG storm, flashing beneath the crawling words: snapshots of keg-stands, parties, and post-game celebrations with buddies; Brody's mean drunk's face and beady, black eyes spiking the camera in each, and everyone. Like he's staring at her from beyond, inside looking out.

Brody 2.0 gets up angry and takes a step towards her, so much like the last time that Genny believes she's dreaming. But when she sees what's crawling around his crotch, the flickers of the videos he made her star in tangled behind the coded letters, numbers, and symbols of his web-girl passwords, her guts freeze in a way that makes her sick. She wonders if any of those videos are still out there, wonders if this is her punishment, if this is the start of a recurring nightmare. All for taking herself back.

"In a minute," she says and walks to the kitchen. So much like the last time, only then she didn't have to think about it, had the benefit of hot anger and fear to push her forwards.

It's a different baseball bat now, the original buried in the woods with the body, but the new one's hidden in the same place, leaning against the wall of the broom closet. As a kid she'd played on a travel team. In high school she went to state. Suffice it to say, she can really swing it. But that's something that the battles took from her, turned what was a lovely tool into something she needed to feel safe. Still needs, because even after it's over, it never really is.

She pours a drink, just like last time, dropping the ice hard so the thing in the den hears it and thinks all is in order. And then she's moving. Her sock-feet landed soft in the beige shag carpet, floating towards the back of it, the head and shoulders floating above the back of the chair, silhouetted by the television's blue ghost light.

She watches Brody 2.0's squirming dome, dark and mannequin-like, tilt back and forth as the thing attempts laughter, squeezing out hissing audio clips of Brody's mocking snort in the direction of the set. Just like last time she thinks as she lines up her knuckles, loads up the bat. A late-night re-run. But of course, it's not.

The bat goes clean through, and instead of cleaning her dead husband's clock Genny topples the brass standing lamp with the angry grind of a car crash. She drops the bat; hands wringing from impact and finds herself staring into the tangled information of The Password Man's chest. With a grunt he lunges, topples over the chair and enfolds her in his arms, and crushes her. She can't breathe. Just like all those times. She can't breathe.

The information enters her, a writhing social security code, a thrashing D.O.B, an undulating passport number. She chokes on his social media profiles. Gags on his travel confirmations. Suffocates on his security questions. **Can you tell us the name of your first pet?** Sure, she thinks, laughing and crying, fighting for life. He had a turtle named Buster, she says aloud, remembering how she'd feed the little box turtle sprigs of lettuce. Brody and Buster together forever. And just like that, Brody 2.0 gasps and the torrent diminishes, ever so slightly. She gropes for another one. **Where was your first date?** Lake Winnipesaukee, a six pack and a canoe. **Your first kiss?** Under the light of the stars and moon.

They come faster. What was your childhood nickname? Butch she recalls, recalling how little it suited him, till it did. **In what city did your parents meet?** Newport.

Brody 2.0 starts screaming and she can feel the pieces of him unlock and disappear, like cords snapping. She gets a breath and stops searching, starts screaming out all she knows about the man who loved and hurt her, feeling like she's pulling out her guts. The Red Sox! Metallica! *The Hunt for Red October!* Halloween! Fall! Rain on the windows! Woodsmoke! The great horned owl!

The screaming becomes something worse, a real death rattle, and she thinks that this is what it should have cost her the first time: this hatred, this sadness.

Code curls away from him like smoke, and she can see light in the place where his heart should be, their wedding video, her and Brody fresh on the other side of eighteen. And she knows why she didn't get rid of the pictures. **The name of the first person you ever loved.**

As the second Brody thins, as his weight evaporates, Genny finds that she's the one holding onto him.

SHUFFLER (DO NO HARM)

July 20th, 2102, 23:40, Carmel Co. Helium And Hydrogen Energy Rig 4 From the recovered audio-log of Janitor Dunk Stephens (Deceased) C.O.D: Unknown. Messy.

There's a shuffler in the station. A strange moving thing that works its way up and down the corridor outside the mess hall, stopping for moments in front of each door. I haven't told anyone yet, I'm not sure if there is anyone left to tell. And besides, I'm not paid to talk about things like that. I'm paid to clean the station, spick and span, and launch bags into space, black for trash, white for recycling, which, now that I think of it, really doesn't matter out here, out here where we just launch it all into the sun and claim victory. That's what I'm here for, annihilating garbage down to the particle. But ever since the Shuffler started doing what it's doing, things have gotten more difficult, mostly because I have to live in the mess hall. Going back to my cabin might involve meeting the Shuffler.

Which I don't want to do. So, I live in the mess hall now, which makes my job difficult, lashing the door shut with some chains I took from the hangar, so that when the Shuffler stops by it doesn't get in. Not that it's tried. It really just stands there,

133

two-foot shadows blocking out the under-door light. Maybe that's all it is, some strange object shaped like under-door foot shadows. Maybe the whole station's filled with them now, standing in front of all the doors, little inch-high black stretches, crawling around on minute tootsies. I'm going to be honest with you here. It's been a while since I left the mess hall.

**

A brief inventory of the things that are keeping me alive physically and spiritually:

Salisbury Steak: 3,476. How? Why?

Water: Theoretically infinite as long as there is power and I have urine.

Power: Infinite. As long as the Sun doesn't fry anything. Sometimes it fries stuff.

Birthday Candles (inedible): 18. Not sure why they're here as we never celebrated any birthdays. And there is no evidence of cake. And why eighteen? Perhaps, a holdover from the previous crew? Perhaps, there were celebrations, and nobody thought to invite me? Stay positive Dunk.

Charcoal biscuits (Inedible): A lot. I'm not going to count them and get all dirty.

'On a Pale Horse' by Piers Anthony (Inedible): My one and only treasure. One picture of bohemian parents (Inedible): 1. Makes me regretful and sad.

One of those dipping bird tchotchkes (inedible): 1. Functional as long as I have water.

Notice of dereliction of duty signed by CPT. Avinash (inedible): 1. Jerk. Received for doing too good of a job. It's not my fault I launched his daughter's poem into the Sun.

Like I told everybody, if you don't want it launched into the Sun don't leave it on the floor.

Lucky half oyster shell that is proving to not be that lucky (inedible): 1.

***

I've drawn my conception of the under-door creature. I had to use napkins and a combination of water and pounded charcoal biscuits to draw so it didn't come out exactly like I had it in my head, but tonight when the Shuffler comes, I'm going to slide it under the hatch as a sort of "are you this thing?" gesture. Now, I do concede that this isn't a foolproof plan, and that I am, perhaps, revealing myself to the Shuffler, which probably has murdered everyone else on the station, otherwise they would have come for me, but I've come to the realization that I simply cannot live in the mess hall for eternity and subsist on what appears to be an endless supply of flash-frozen Salisbury steaks. I am so, so tired of Salisbury steak. And I left the rest of my Piers Anthony in my cabin. I guess what I'm saying is that this isn't really living and I don't want to do it without Piers. All right I hear it now, I'm going to initiate the experiment.

***

Okay, well, I slid the picture of the under-door creature, you know the concept of the foot shadows as an actual physical rubbery animal thing? Well, I'm pretty sure the Shuffler noticed it because it moaned for a while, than shrieked for a while, then made some sort of undulating warbling for a while, and then slid the drawing back under the hatch to me, covered with some kind of green slime rune which either means, "Nice to meet you, I'm not going to murder you," or, "Boy, I can't wait to murder you." Honestly, it's hard to interpret anything that's going on.

Maybe none of this is going on? Well, that's a stretch. You know, maybe the Shuffler was asking a question. Maybe it thought I was an under-door creature, that I had drawn a picture of myself? Because if it looks that way to me, I probably look that way to it.

***

I have another theory as to why nobody is coming to get me. Perhaps, instead of being murdered by the Shuffler they simply evacuated and forgot about me? Which would go hand-and-hand with me never being invited to any of the birthday parties that might have occurred. Of course, there is always the possibility that no birthday parties occurred, and I am simply being oversensitive. Is it bad to hope that everybody died instead of forgetting about me? It's bad.

I wonder if my bohemian parents are still alive. Before I left for space, my mother told me I was sending myself to the corner. That was my punishment when I was a kid. To stand in the corner. My dad would hold a kitchen timer by my ear as an additional wrinkle of punishment. I miss them.

I think, when you're trapped in a mess hall by what may be a vicious alien menace, it's important to feel as many different emotions as possible so as to not to go crazy. So, I'm glad I've got this photo, which makes me feel horrible whenever I look at it.

***

I've decided to test the Shuffler's intelligence with a rudimentary trash experiment. I've written an approximation of a math equation on a napkin using charcoal paste concerning the precise weight limits necessary when launching trash into the vacuum of space. You know, it's really not a math problem.

136

I don't know why I said that. It's basically a cave painting of me throwing garbage from a Colonial-style window lodged in the side of the doughnut-shaped station. It's of course not realistic, as we have no colonial style windows, but I couldn't accurately depict what the station windows actually look like. I don't think window is even the correct term in space. Anyway, here it comes again, I'm going to initiate the experiment.

***

Okay, well that was a waste of time and charcoal paste. Once again, the Shuffler decided to puke symbols all over the drawing I spent a very long time making. I'm not upset. I'm not. But I think it's rude. A little rude. Especially if the Shuffler has killed everyone. In that case I'm dealing with a very unsavory character who could've just pretended to like my drawing.

Anyhow, I think the root of the problem is a lack of basic understanding. I'm going to try to create a shared alphabet for the two of us to communicate with, or rather a simple way for IT to understand MY alphabet.

Let's see here, I'll start by…how… do I… do this? Hmmmm…. Morse code! That's it. I'll teach it Morse code, my own special version because I don't know Morse code, aside from the beeps and the dashes. I'll simplify it. Only beeps! No dashes! So, one beep for A. Two for B. Three for C. Four for D. Five for E. Six for F. Seven for G and so on. Here it comes! I'm going to initiate the experiment.

***

So, I shouldn't have started with "Who are you?" because the W alone was twenty-three beeps and by the time I finished beeping the Shuffler had finished screaming and was gone. I don't think my beep alphabet is a fully functioning idea. How's the Shuffler supposed to know what an A is to begin with? Or a B! Or a C! Or a D for that matter! I think I'm getting hysterical. Oh my God I'm trapped in here, I'm actually trapped in here...

Maybe I could do one beep for yes and two for no... That's a better start. Or I could just stick with pictures, something simple. A happy face and a sad face. A sick face and healthy face. A face eating questionable Salisbury steak and a face puking it all up into a series of strange alphabetic signatures.

There is always the final solution. Always the opening of the door and saying hello. Here it comes. I've got my faces ready, they're simplistic and I don't think I've got the contours of the Salisbury streak and the puke just right, but it'll have to do. Here let me circle the one that represents how I feel. The puke face. Dear Shuffler, I feel like a puke face.

***

Apparently, the Shuffler feels like all the faces as it puked a slime rune on each and every drawing and slid them back. Perhaps, it is trying to teach me IT'S alphabet! I will say that it's a very corrosive alphabet. I got a little bit on the tip of my finger and it burned the skin right off. As it stands, I'm simply accumulating an acidic pile of garbage in the corner of the mess hall.

Which, sooner or later, may or may not burn a hole through the hull and eject me into the vacuum of space and into the Sun. Which is the most poetic demise that I can think of.

Regardless, I think I'd like to avoid it.

My bohemian parents must be so disappointed with me. If they're not dead. They wanted me to be an artist. Or a rock star. Any kind of creative genius. And instead I chose to do nothing. To be nothing. I chose the simplest, most non-offensive occupation in the entire universe. But that was the point. I think I'm being too hard on myself. I think I'm too hard on myself. I INVENTED a way of producing charcoal paste! That's something.

***

If this experience has taught me anything it is this inarguable rule of the universe: If left alone for long enough, a Dunk will find a way to create charcoal paste.

***

Because I have literally nothing else to do besides attempt communication with a possible alien menace, I've decided to make physical contact with the Shuffler. I've got four pairs of latex dishwashing gloves on so I should be okay if I get slimed. Whatever happens at least I'll know how hostile it is. Here it comes! I'll just slip my fingers under the hatch and wiggle them a bit and…WOW! That feels…different. OUCH! There's a great deal of pressure…and… suction… and…feels like each of my fingers is in a separate orifice that…really, really enjoys it being there…I don't think I'm comfortable with this anymore…

***

I have two theories about what just happened. A: The Shuffler tried to eat my fingers. B: The Shuffler made earnest sexual intercourse with my fingers. Regardless it's a good thing I had protection. Unfortunately, the gloves are now smoldering in the acid pile and I am no closer to understanding if I'm dealing with an enemy. How does one do this? How do I communicate with a living thing that isn't a living thing I'm used to? What would a scientist do? A linguist? What would

Piers Anthony do? These are the things I need to know and don't. I should have paid attention in school. Or school should have paid more attention to me. I should have made choices that didn't result in living in the orbit of the sun, launching garbage into it with impunity. I should have worked at a bird hospital with those monks that refuse to step on bugs.

***

My first girlfriend humiliated me when I didn't know the difference between your and 'you're. I was twenty-four. I am completely unqualified for anything, especially this.

***

I realize, as the Shuffler now moans and warbles at my door, that the one thing I have not tried to do is talk to it. Most of my attempts at communication have been non-verbal or non- sensical. Perhaps, I am overthinking things. Perhaps, all it needs is to hear my voice. Like a horse that needs a friendly voice.

While I cannot know if the Shuffler is a threat to me, I can know that I am not a threat to it. I can decide that. To not bash it over the head with the fire extinguisher. That's an okay thing. To not be a threat. That's a hard thing for a person to do. Listen to me Shuffler, here is how and why I came to be a janitor in space: When I was a kid, before I squandered my opportunities and became a disappointment, I spent my summers in the Chesapeake Bay with my wealthy bohemian parents. Across the water, in the parts of Delaware nobody was using anymore, I could see the great shapes of starships under construction. The clouds of greasy smog their construction necessitated blanketed the sky in a constant green-grey swirl, coated the choppy Atlantic whitecaps with greasy rainbows.

Our neighbor was a leather skinned, Speedo-wearing old man whom the neighborhood kids knew as Dr. Dove. He was a former software executive living out his days in self-imposed exile after the company he chaired defrauded billions of clients in a global financial collapse.

As penance he farmed oysters. Day and night. Trudging up and down his rickety docks in the windswept, tropical swelter of late twenty-first century Maryland. And that was all there was to him. All that was left. His oysters and his speedos.

He didn't sell his oysters, rather he used their filtering powers in a tragicomic attempt to purify the putrid bay. No quantity of oysters were capable of doing this, so he simply accumulated more and more till his estuaries became a series of small, then large reefs that obstructed personal watercraft. One of those reefs eventually killed a famous football player on a jet-ski joyride.

Each day at lunch I watched Dr. Dove from the fringes of his property, our two lawns mismatched squares of green, his sickly and near yellow: ours thick, emerald and forest-like. Back and forth he'd go, back and forth, from his house to his estuaries all hours of the day, a madman in a Speedo, muttering under his breath. And I'd just watch, a distant little shadow munching on a ham sandwich.

The day the football player died, the day before he was arrested for manslaughter, crazy Dr. Dove spoke to me. He was walking back from his docks cradling something in his hands. He shouted something unintelligible at the sky and fell to his knees. The way he was kneeling, the way his old skin folded over itself, made it impossible to see that he was wearing a speedo. Do you know what he looked like, Shuffler? He looked like a sad, naked old man. He looked like a Gob. He looked like how I imagine I look now.

From my patch of luscious green grass, I called to him.

"Are you okay?" I asked. He looked up and muttered at me and at nothing. Then muttered the same thing only louder and crazier. Then he got up and lumbered towards me and made me pee my pants a little. From a few feet away, I could see that his eyes were rheumy and yellow and not-at-all healthy looking. He spoke again, clearly this time, in a way that seemed to explain the mysteries of existence. He said, "I am the destroyer of worlds." Then he placed a dead oyster at my feet and went back out into the bay and inadvertently murdered a professional athlete.

What he said was a quote from a famous dead person who helped invent a way to kill the world. That's how Dr. Dove saw himself, because despite trying to create good, all he created was a way to kill oysters.

The next day, when they took him away, ranting and screaming and mostly naked, I looked at the starships in the distance and decided that there wasn't much left to do where I was. I decided that if I was going to do something pointless, I was going to do it far, far away. I still have the oyster, a putrid reminder of how to do no harm in the world. To do no harm is to do nothing.

It took me a couple of days to realize that it wasn't a rock, but a thing that had once been alive. Maybe that's what they'll think about me when they find my digested bones. Here are the remains of a nobody that used to be alive.

***

Last night, after hearing my story, the Shuffler proceeded to knock on the mess hall door twenty-three times, which, as you may recall, is the symbol for W. So, there is hope. There is hope for peace.

***

I'm going to unchain the door, and wait, wait for the creature that is either my friend or foe, with enough Salisbury steak for the both of us and all eighteen candles. It may not understand me, I may not understand it, but it will understand kindness. Anything can understand kindness. And so, I am throwing the Shuffler a birthday party.

I think I left Earth because I wasn't the right person to do anything. To help anything. So, I went someplace where what I did didn't matter. Now here, on the eve of first contact, with no expertise in anything, I find myself to be the exact perfect person for the job.

Thank you, Dr. Dove. If I escape. Not if. WHEN I escape. I'm going to retire to Chesapeake Bay. And I'll farm oysters like you did. Not for the bay mind you, but for the oysters.

Here it comes, I'm going to light the candles, I'm going to initiate the birthday party.

End Log Delete? Y/N

Deliver to next of kin: One-half oyster shell, one copy *'On a Pale Horse'*.

WAVE TO THE SPACEMAN

I see it in the red distance, a thing discarded. My town. A
fuzzy pile on the darkening horizon, sliver of gibbous moon
peeking up over the old water tower. The sky above, it's
another planet, the cosmic band of milky way stretching
through a cloud of glittering purple-green fungal spores,
descending in spiral-like fingertips, hands coming to wipe it
all off the earth. Old heads say the spores came from the food,
poison on an earth-wide scale, exhaled into the atmosphere
by tomatoes and eggplants, twinkling down to kill us all like
manna from heaven. Sounds ridiculous. Is ridiculous. But
you've got to trust the old heads. Or pretend to. They've got the
longest memories. All the way back from when people had the
expectation of living without disaster.

Wonder what that was like? Wonder if anyone finds the
urge to keep on keeping on anymore. I do. My girls. I measure
my interest in living by how many throats I slit. Counting on
two hands now. Kids got to eat.

Yet still I'm doing this. Testing my fate, which is testing
theirs. Sneaking into my town like I do most nights, twins
wrapped up tight in their make-shift spacesuits, asleep in our
truck-bed wagon, clear tarp overhead so they can see what's

killing them. What am I looking for?

Aside from canned peaches. I know. Of course I know. What I buried in the backyard.

Passing the perimeter, Jerry gives me his customary greeting. Tells me he'll shoot if I take another step. Poor, quaking little teenage boy, rifle's more than half his body. I've done a guard before, digit six of seven, pinned it on a glow easy, but I won't do little Jerry. It's not his fault. Old heads say nobody leaves. Not that anyone cares anymore. Caravan's dying more and more each day since it stopped moving, people and families dropping out of their spacesuits and heading into the horizon, back home, or someplace new, inviting the spores through each and every pore. Not fighting. Not fighting must be nice.

Half a mile out, I think I can still hear the lonesome gargle of Jerry crying through his rebreather. Poor kid. Just wants to be a man with a gun. Maybe he will shoot me one of these days. I look back, the lights of the caravan twinkling, cook fires quavering with smoke, a broken constellation of weak quasars, destined to get smaller and smaller. Funny how it stopped here, right here outside of where I grew up, smoked cigarettes, broke bottles and got pregnant in the back of a Silverado. Fate. Hardly. There's only so much of the southwest to wander around before you double back, that is when all you're doing is doubling, marching like the exodus without a pot to piss in. No Moses, neither. That's something I ask myself a lot, in this strange end of the world. Where did all the Moses' go? Weren't we due at least one?

I take off my fishbowl helmet to smoke a stale cigarette. Been doing this more and more. Old heads be damned. Not much use to living if you don't do it right from time to time. I walk in dark, spore dust kicking up with every step of my heavy boots, scents of salt and cinnamon swirling into my nostrils.

The desert is a dry, black-light cosmic spread, and I plow through it like a giant, each dune of lambent accumulation a galaxy. It's tremendous. Up ahead, between me and my town, there's a coyote frozen in mid-step, spine protruding in an arch, proud with three rainbow tomatoes heart-beating; puffing out green, purple and gold dust onto the dead animal's hide. Terraforming, or something, I'd guess. No. Not dead. I get closer and see the tongue is still lolling around those idiot canines. This is how it is, you die, but you don't really, more like you go vegetable, literal and figurative. I squat to meet the animal eye-level and give its chin a scratch.

There's a glo sitting on a folding chair nearby, watching the coyote like it's a campfire.

Young guy in mesh shorts and a Diamondbacks jersey, skin painted with phosphorescence, backwards hat moldering into his scalp. In his decay he looks like a deep-sea creature, smiling at me like a happy, little idiot. There's people back at the caravan who'd kill him on principle. Used to be, I was one.

"Complete nutrition." He says by way of hello, teeth mossy and glowing, "Part of a complete breakfast." Say what you will about the infected, they sure are friendly. He points at the coyote fruits, which look about as good as Garden of Eden apples. Smell even better, like fresh waffles and honey. Fuck, I remember waffles.

"No thanks." I say, measuring my resistance.

The glo bows his head and nods, giving me a nice look at the ball of his neck. He's starting to sprout too.

"What's it like?" I ask, "Being one of you?"

Guy shrugs, gesticulates to the coyote, to the firmament around us, "80 percent lean. twenty percent fat. Most times. Grass fed and never antibiotics." He narrows his eyes, slick with rainbow sheen, looks deep into my soul like he's on the verge of the massive, "Air chilled...free range." He says, like it's an admission, "Never lonely though."

He goes back to staring at the coyote. I stare too, watching the creature's flanks shudder and gleam, a pearlescent, dog shaped aurora against the velvety purple of the not-quite-dark. I put my helmet back on. It's never fully dark anymore.

***

I step from the hard-pan directly onto the cracked concrete of main-street, same stone I skinned knees on years ago. Power's back on in town, marque over the diner launching an idolatry of halogen fries into the cosmos. Might be the glo-sticks reconnected it. I feel like a space-invader with my suit on, some stranger touched down from another planet, rebreather pumping dead air around my lungs. I was a queen here. Travel team point guard and cheer captain. Never in my dreams did I think I'd come back as a wasteland throat-cutter.

There're people. More than last time. Reverse-refugees moving back, settling down and sharing yard fences with the infected, killing time before they join them. A kid plays catch with a terrier, two shucks of corn growing from the dog's side. Got to be some folks from the caravan, not that I know too many faces, hard to learn the look of someone through a hazmat visor. They watch me from their porches cracking knowing smiles that make me nervous, faces caked in spores, sci-fi dust bowl Americana. As long as I'm in the suit, I'm not one of them. Still a survivor. Yet why do I feel so close? Roots of course. Buried in the backyard. In me. No matter how many murders or apocalypses, this place still feels mine. This blacklight carnival. It's beautiful. The Walmart, an emerald monolith turned stall market, snowy blue parking lot dotted with barkers selling fruit that smells like barbecued lamb, cotton candy, and bourbon; cook-fires eating up the bioluminescent fog. Is this the way the world ends, or how it begins?

***

The house we bought sits in the darkness at the edge of town, a ranchero, small and dim next to the riot of downtown. Some aspiring artists have used the darkness to their advantage, using spore dust to paint the block with glowing serpents, dragons and winged graffities. The block, an illustrated children's book with admirable three-point perspective.

There's a caravan-family I used to trade with over in the neighboring house, eating dinner in the living room. Kids, a girl and a boy with names I never bothered to learn, still lean with survival meanness, but getting softer, cheeks already pearlescent with glow. Happy together. Never mind the strange apocalypse outside. I watch them from my trash cans, and they wave at me, whatever I've become. Numbers two through four I popped with a rifle for fun in the early days of the caravan. My God. How I used to believe.

Inside the house, it's sad. Moldering and blue-dark, coffin still, air swirling against my movements with dim, dead particulate, the untouched decay of the family-life I thought would last forever. I remember you, husband, walking through these halls after our shot-gun wedding, ruddy-faced and eager to make it. So much of this house remains untouched, kettle on the stove, pictures on the wall layered to obscurity by dead skin. Husband's football trophies and my cheer ones. Goddamn, we were American.

I remember you, husband, your running-back footfalls chasing the kids. You and me, the king and queen of the prom, slow dancing naked to *Racing in the Street*. Then the world got strange, and I remember you, husband, standing in the doorway of our bedroom holding onto the frame like Atlas, shambling and glow-eyed, babbling out nonsense and scaring our babies, alien fruits and vegetables pushing to get out of your skin like foreign organs. You became number one that way. Because I thought it was a mercy, or I was too scared to feel otherwise. I wonder how you felt about it. That straight razor left to right. You smiled the whole time.

"We grow." You said, "We grow and grow."

I buried you in the yard. Which is how I know, the caravan dying here, it's not fate. It's gravity. Bringing us back to where we should have stayed.

I take my helmet off and drop it onto the cheap, ancient shag, where it thuds in deep, rolls once and goes still, already finding its place in the decay. There aren't any spores here, I'm safe, if that word still applies, but it's still not a place to strip naked, which is what I do. Not exactly pleasant standing au natural in this box of aerosol skin, but it's a damn sight fresher than being locked in a spacesuit for nigh on years. I unfold the suit next to the helmet, arranging myself a skinned cosmonaut on the floor. Wave to the spaceman. This is erratic behavior, is what this is. I go to our old bedroom and I find myself a dress, stale and moth eaten, hanging loose against my sharp and evil ribs.

Outside in the garden I can see the stars clear, a pocket of true human night overhead.

Might be the last time I ever see such a thing. The grass has regrown, dark green and impossibly thick. I curl my toes into it and squeeze, digging the cool earth. Husband's shallow grave has sprouted a thicket, green stalks curling their way upwards into shapes that look like letters, letters that look like words. I take a look at what I've been coming to check, how the grass above his body is moving, like something breathing again down there, rustling the green stalks into susurrations.

I lie down on top, bury my face into the earth and breathe deep. "See you soon." I whisper.

***

Back in the desert, the coyote is still there. Panting and eye-rolling, spine arching out of its back. The spores underfoot chill my toes and I think that I should have at least kept the boots. I kneel and give the wolf-dog another chin scratch, placing my forehead against its, and think of my girls, as I find the glowing fruits growing from its bones and remove them. Three in total, one for each of us.

Free from its burden, the coyote leans against its paws and stretches, its exposed spine sliding back to where it's supposed to be. The animal trots away into the glamoured dark and hovers, yips twice and trots back, mouthing at my hand for a few more caresses. I give the animal's mouth my three fingers on the right hand, the three that don't match any dead people. Let the creature work at them playfully. The caravan twinkles in the outer dark, its weak light struggling against the shimmer of this alien dawn, the two canceling each other out so as to make both look dull. There are some fights we're not supposed to win, I guess.

My left-hand clamps around the coyote's snout, willing it to bite. The slice of pain means the critter gets the idea. Good boy. Two hands are too many, and you can't live soul rotten, even if you might not live at all.

THE SNEAKABOO

I bought the walrus at the carnival off I-95. The one that sets up in the lot next to the Carvel every August. And I say bought because I couldn't knock over a physically impossible pyramid of soup cans. My wife whispered "pussy" into my ear and squeezed my butt a bit too hard for it to be funny. So, while she and Jackson were spinning in the teacups, I doubled back and slipped the carnie a twenty. Then I went cock-walking back with a big grin on my face, windmilling my throwing arm, a spaniel-sized walrus tucked behind my back, Windex blue with a pink Santa hat stitched on crooked. For Jackson it was love at first sight.

I said I won it, and to this day Meg doesn't know any different. It remains one of the great secrets of our marriage. I'm proud that she thinks I earned it. But I bought it. And I wish to God that I hadn't. Because for a summer it ran our life, and so did Jackson, who was an imperious little shit around that time. And I know this is something all parents say. But for us it was true. It really was. Because when we didn't do what Jackson wanted, Sneakaboo got upset. And that's why my nose looks the way it does. That and the frying pan.

***

Sneakaboo got its name on the drive back. Jackson was refusing to get into his car seat, wanting to ride the walrus like a horse instead. I said it was okay. Because forty-five minutes of screaming is too much. And it was okay, 'til I got pulled over by a state trooper and lost five hundred dollars and a point off my license.

While I was busy learning about parental neglect, Meghan did her best to distract Jackson, using the walrus for a game of peak-a-boo, only Jackson regurgitated it as, "Sneakaboo! Sneakaboo." Which, I'll admit, was a little heart-melting. At the time.

That was one of the last good days. With a difficult child, you have to count those. To hold on, because you have to remind yourself that it's worth it. Because when you're shit deep, the shit's the only reality, and those memories are the proof that it was better and can be again. That you do, in fact, love your children.

Look, I'll admit, I wasn't always the best dad. I got angry. Meg's always been the one to remind me that you can't yell at a child the same way you yell at an adult. Or a teenager. You're really not supposed to yell at anyone. But Jackson would have these meltdowns, over nothing, just nothing, and I'd blow my lid. I'd call him spoiled. Tell him how different it was for me. All that.

I still don't know if we ever did the right things with him. Maybe he needed a little fear of God. Maybe things would have been different. I don't know. I don't think Meg does either, though she'll never admit it. Little Hurricane Jackson is what we called him back then. Our little hurricane Jackson.

That night, Jackson insisted on having Sneakaboo in his crib. Which scared me, because I'd heard stuff about kids smothering themselves. But he screamed. And Meg did that thing that made her right about everything and me wrong about everything and we all went to bed angry and nobody had sex. Then it got weird.

***

The next morning, Meg came in to wake me with a look on her face. She sat on the corner of the bed and stared into space and put a finger to her lower lip and pulled it a little. For a second I thought that I was right, finally right, that our son had died in his crib, face down in a carnival prize. Then I heard Jackson squeal in his room down the hallway, and Meghan looked at me like she was going to say something, but didn't.

Sneakaboo had doubled in size overnight, fluff bursting from its ruptured seams in white gouts, the protruding cotton bulbous and gnarled like fungal growths. The face is what got me. It had torn free from the rest of the fabric, a buttoned-eyed blue circle floating on an extended neck protrusion of coarse cotton. Its mouth, a little curly-cue of black stitches, drooping from a spade of a nose that fused into tusked jowls. The whole countenance screwed together into a pink- cheeked squint-smile. I'm telling you it was Michael Myers-esque. Real dead-eyed.

Jackson wouldn't let me take it from him, wouldn't let me look at it. And when I tried, he screamed, and I swear the thing shuddered.

Meg thought it was bedbugs, that the carnie had given it to me as payback for winning at his rigged game, which of course I hadn't. Or for being upper middle class. I didn't say anything to dissuade her. Anything seemed better than telling her that it had moved.

I floated going back and pressing the carnie, and she pounced on the idea. So, I took a few hours while Meg went about distracting Sneakaboo away from Jackson, a tactic that involved pints of ice cream. I want to add here that it's not like we spoiled the kid because we were lazy.

This was just how he was. He got angry, he got scared, and it drove him nuts. Just nuts. And after hours and days we had to give in. There was no choice. No improving him. We checked. We did tests. All I know is that he wasn't happy, and that he hated it as much as we did.

***

So, I go to the carnival and, what do you know? Thing's gone. Packed up and disappeared. Just an empty lot of bad grass, tinged and bald where the big machines had rubbed it away.

I smoked a cigarette without fear of getting caught and counted the weeds, the little drug bags. I walked to the exact spot where I thought the stall was and just stood there, waiting for revelation. It was a nice day, and the cars on the highway whistled past, and all together it was a pleasant break from being a dad. There's something profound in standing where a carnival once was, a mystery to how all that neon bustle went poof.

I went to the Carvel and got some strawberry ice cream.

***

When I got back, Jackson was watching cartoons in an ice cream coma. *Courage the Cowardly Dog*, I think. Meg was poring over Sneakaboo with a magnifying glass, bug hunting. She'd over-invested at this point. As scary as the whole thing got, parts of it excited her. She loves this kind of stuff. Horror movie stuff.

I wrapped my arms around her neck and smelled her head and we watched the rest of the show in silence.

"No bug," she said. "No carnie," I said.

By bedtime we'd decided that we were crazy, that the walrus was poorly made, that we just hadn't noticed that it was as big as a Saint Bernard between the tantrum and the highway stop.

We tucked Jackson in alongside his monstrosity and watched him sleep. I was happy that I had given him something that he was in love with.

***

It was not an uncommon occurrence for Jackson to wake us up in the middle of the night with outrageous demands. That night was no different, only he didn't come alone. As Jackson toddled into our room like he owned the place, Sneakaboo came loping in after him. It had grown again, sprouted huge muscular arms of cotton that it used to knuckle itself forward, dragging its walrus bulk behind it.

Meg screamed and scrambled towards the headboard, pulling her legs to her chest in a frenzy of sheets.

"Holy shit." I think I said.

I got up, knocked over my bedside lamp and stood there with my fists up.

"Gwilled cheese." Jackson squeaked, bouncing his hands on the mattress in his little boy way, not reading the room at all. Sneakaboo slouched behind him, vibrating, head weaving on that too-long neck, shredded blue face impassive and wrong, tusks undulating like roach antennae. That was the worst part. The part that still gets me nauseous. Those fucking tusks.

"Gwilled Cheese." Jackson said again, then again and again. "Gwilled Cheese! Gwilled Cheese! Gwilled Cheese!"

"Holy shit." I probably reiterated. Inside I was going, *No. No. No. No. No. This is not a thing that is happening.*

At this point, having not gotten what he wanted, Jackson decided that it was time for all hell to break loose. He started screaming. Not crying, screaming. Angry and wild. Meghan started moaning and I looked at her and she was just tearing the sheets, trying to pull them into her body. I looked back towards Jackson and the Sneakaboo was pulling itself towards me, loping on those massive fists. I was still going, *No. No. No. This is very obviously not a real thing that's happening. It's got a stupid Santa hat. Look at that stupid Santa hat. It's summer.*

Then it reached me, put me in a headlock and threw me to the shag carpet. Never let anyone tell you shag carpet is a bad thing. Shag carpet might have saved my life that night. Because that monster started pummeling me, and wouldn't you know it? Those fluffy fists felt like rocks.

I crawled away from the beating, bloody and bruised, and somehow, I don't remember how, made my son a fucking grilled cheese sandwich.

***

How do I describe this next part? Our son came into possession of a magical creature that amplified his tantrums into moments of real physical danger. So yeah, it sucked. And neither of us knew what to do. And the things we did try resulted in beatings, in being flung across the room into walls. Resulted in concussions and bone bruises and staggered visits to our doctor who gave us each a very impassioned speech about domestic violence.

So, for survival's sake we maintained a hands-off policy

at first. We watched our son play with his monster from doorways, from the top of the stairs; quietly swooping in if he couldn't open a peanut butter jar.

Much to our surprise Jackson could largely exist without our involvement, living off toilet water and boxes of cereal. But he still needed us. He still fell flat on his face and cried at the injustice of it all. Still needed a bedtime story to fall asleep. The only thing the Sneakaboo had for him then was rage, thrashing blindly as Jackson howled in misery. Our son still loved us. Still wanted us. He just had the ability to overpower us and didn't understand what that meant.

So, we got back in there. We had to. And, that meant getting beaten up whenever Jackson's mood would swing during a diaper change.

The worst part was when Jackson forced us to play with Sneakaboo, to willingly wrestle with the horrifying creature and act like we were in on the joke and not shitting ourselves stupid. I cried the first few times. I hadn't cried since I was a kid, not even when my dad died, but I did then, and not like a man, not like a grown-up. I cried like a child. I whimpered. I wet myself. I mean, I thought it was going to kill me. Every time Sneakaboo put me in a headlock at the behest of our little boy emperor, I waited to hear the sound of my neck snapping. And then, slobbering and humiliated, I had to watch my wife do the same.

I don't know how we made it. I guess we got used to it, but those first few times, smashed into that penny-store monster's brittle fur… the feeling, the horror. The way it moved, always dead-eyed, animal and inanimate at the same time, those tusks always going, flickering, the one part of the creature that didn't feel like it came from Jackson but from somewhere else, beyond the pale.

Look, back then, and I don't mean to brag, I mean why would I, but back then, I did my husbandly duty. I took every beating I could to spare Meg. Volunteered myself for every play session. And when I couldn't go on, when I was about to tag-out and slit my wrists, she did the same for me.

When you have a kid your affection, your bone loyalty latches on to them, and as a result you lose a little of what you had for your spouse. That's what had happened with me and Meg when Jackson was born. We both loved him, so, so much. But when Sneakaboo came on the scene that loyalty flipped back. Meg and I were always in the trenches together, always consoling each other, and it was like when we were in college.

Our bodies told each other what we were giving to our marriage every night, as long as we both weren't too exhausted. It felt safe, being so clearly on the same team, even if we were never too far from our son's silent enforcer.

And as we got used to the pain, it started getting funny. I mean, it was just, so, so ridiculous. It was a walrus in a Santa hat. If there's one thing life has taught me, it is that there is not a single horrifying thing that cannot be made less so by the addition of a Santa hat. What did horrify me was that I started to hate Jackson. I started to hate my son.

***

After a few weeks, things started moving towards normalization, or rather to a form of it. It was all a matter of anticipating Jackson's needs and preparing to distract him when his mood went sour. I quit my job. We slept in shifts so we could have the grilled cheese ready before he started wondering where it was. I ordered a mini fridge to keep ice cream in his bedroom and hid cookies in strategic locations. The point was to always have a plan. And it worked. Most of the time. But it wasn't ideal. He still was making all the decisions. Plus, he was getting obese, which the pediatrician would give us the eyebrows for if we ever made it out of the house again.

But the system gave us time to make plans. To think about how to get rid of Sneakaboo.

We thought about calling the cops, but were afraid they might take Jackson away from us. Meghan was worried that the government would experiment on him, or put him on television. Which sounds like something the government might do, I guess.

We considered our options, covered the fridge with the numbers of priests and parapsychologists. But in our hearts, we knew, or maybe hoped, that there were no answers outside our four walls. It was just our son that was happening to us, the unknowable piece of him just outside of our reach, the hurricane. And if we could find the eye of it, we could will him towards normalcy. Of course, there was also the issue of being seen, of being judged, of being liable, the implication that our son's mental control over a violent and impossible monstrosity might somehow reflect poorly on our parenting.

What became apparent was that our time was not infinite. We made calls, cancelled nana's visit, told friends that Jackson was suffering from something deeply contagious, but sooner or later the time shut away would become weird. Then it was only a matter of when, not if, child services showed up at our door. In America, you can't simply disappear your kids, not after the grid knows about them.

In the end the thing that made sense was fire. To simply wait till Jackson was passed out and torch the fucking thing. Unfortunately, Jackson usually slept in Sneakaboo's arms, huddled into that strange mass of blue and white froth like a chimp baby, which made me jealous to no end. But it didn't always happen that way: every now and then the kid passed out in a pile of empty ice cream pints like an adorable little drunk, leaving the Sneakaboo inert and vulnerable, except for those tusks.

***

Fire poker. Rag. Chemical log. One bucket of gasoline. A place where I couldn't burn the house to cinders. The silver buckle belt my father gave me on my twenty-first birthday. One black burlap sack. That's what it took. I'll never forgive myself for the last one. I know Jackson doesn't, even if he can't remember. Speaking of which, black burlap is hard to find and hard to buy without oozing guilt. Got it at the hardware store across the highway from the Carvel. How do you want to see the world?

It was a Sunday night, August seventeenth. I made sure I was drunk enough to feel mean, sober enough to act. Meghan was upstairs crying herself to sleep. Sneakaboo, that big blue fuck, had torn out a piece of her scalp while she was reading a book to Jackson and stretched his patience too far. So yeah, I felt mean. I felt good and mean.

I lured Jackson to the basement with ice cream sandwiches, doing my best to stay out of sight. One sandwich at the top of the stairs, one at the bottom. One down the hall. One at the top of the basement stairs. If this plan seems strange or odd, I was pretty much half-insane. I was shirtless. I thought I was Rambo. But it worked. I watched from the shadows as my son followed my trail, the Sneakaboo hulking behind him, a cheap monstrosity loping through the columns of moonlight that barreled through the windows, my little black-haired boy leading him along, ragged and long-haired like one of those kids raised by wolves.

When I was sure he was following, I crept ahead to the basement. We had an old CRT TV down there hooked up to a VCR. I pressed play on *Fievel Goes West,* Jackson's favorite, and turned the sound up. I've yet to meet the toddler that won't cross deserts to follow the sounds of a distant cartoon.

I hid out of sight, flattened between the wall and the open

basement door, my fire poker held tight, wrapped to the point with gasoline-soaked rags and chemical-log skin, primed to become a flaming spear at the stroke of a match. The bucket of gasoline lay at my feet. The idea was to set the creature on fire and then keep it burning, but to do that I needed Jackson out of the way.

From the top of the stairs my son called to me, "Ada? Addy?" His versions of dad and daddy.

"Down here, buddy." I called to him, my heart trying to punch its way into my throat. "Come watch cartoons with Daddy."

He squealed and started clomping down the stairs, which I realized he shouldn't be doing by himself. I checked the impulse to run to him, reminded myself that he wasn't alone, that he had his own profane interloper that was stealing all my fatherly moments. I lit the poker. And God forgive me for this next part, when Jackson emerged, happy and messy with ice cream plastered to his face, I stepped out from behind, covered his head with my burlap bag, tied the belt around his neck and flung him away. Again, I am so, so sorry for this last part. Definitely a low parenting moment for me.

Things happened quickly after that. Jackson screamed, screeched really, burning out his last good breath on a whine pitchy enough to make my eyes swim. And Sneakaboo went berserk, started smashing and twirling without a target, blinded without Jackson being able to identify the source of his unhappiness.

I went for my gasoline bucket and caught a flipper-fist that broke my jaw and sent a tooth skittering. That was almost the end right there. I dropped to the ground; half my face wrapped towards the back of my head. Through bloody fingers I saw my boy, tugging at his neck, clawing, and that gave me all the wind I needed. I struggled up, bucket in hand, turned to the rampaging walrus thing, the creature eerily soundless in its fury, and doused it in gasoline. The Sneakaboo didn't so much as flinch: no recognition, no animal reaction to being soaked in the pungent grease. I balked for a second, one final second, picturing my son burning alive, then I stabbed my burning poker into Sneakaboo's fluffy guts and set that fucker to fry. It went up in an eye-blink, the gasoline a spreading blue ripple, riding a whooshing sigh that tingled my spine.

There was no noise, no noise in all that chaos. Sneakaboo thrashed like a silent movie Frankenstein as it twirled into ashes, launching droplets of fire in all directions, almost beautiful.

Jackson choked out a groan like a squashed toad and I remembered what I had done. He was on the ground contorting his little body, bucking his spine in a way no child should, blood trickling down his shirt front.

I grabbed him bodily around the waist and hauled him up the stairs, straight into Meg, ragged and unkempt in her flannel pajamas. She looked at my bloodied face, then at our son trussed up and bagged like a shot deer, back to me. Then she hit me in the head with a frying pan.

**

I'm not going to ask for sympathy. I believe in what I did, although perhaps not in the way I did it. Frying pans are just what happens when you make a unilateral parenting decision. The pain was bad. Struggling into consciousness to see my son foaming at the mouth in his mother's arms was worse. I watched him spit out the tip of his tongue into her lap. Just the very tip. He lived. He's not rolling his R's or anything, but he lived.

Meg gathered him up in her arms and took him out into

the night, to what I later learned was the hospital.

For a while I thought I was going to die, slumped there at the top of the basement stairs, all beat the fuck up, choking on burning stuffed animal and gasoline. But I didn't die. The fire burned itself out, suffocated in the concrete tomb that was our basement.

The cops didn't come. Neither did the fire department. If they had, I don't think we'd have survived. As a family, I mean. I don't know why. The whole thing sure felt loud, felt out of hand in the way that attracts neighbors. But aside from my son's single scream, I suppose it was all silent; just a little darkness in the fringes of suburbia, out where there's still a little woods to get lost in.

The ambulance didn't come either, so I can assume that around that time Meg didn't care if I lived or died. I don't blame her, but I can't say I don't hold it against her.

***

I spent two days drinking water from the toilet, eating from the torn bags of cereal Jackson had left around the house. Like father, like son.

Eventually I got to my feet and went to the basement. The floor where Sneakaboo had burned was scorched deep black, beautiful brushstrokes of char, the cork tiling whirled and swirled, melted and reformed into alien ripples. It looked like a spiral galaxy of black and brown, twisting towards an ever-dark center of carbon, and a bubblegum pink, lightly singed Santa hat.

I put the hat on. It smelled like caramel. I put it on and went to the CRT (which, remarkably, was in perfect working order) and watched *Fievel Goes West* in its entirety. Twice.

Then I went out and staged a car crash to explain my injuries.

***

When you hold your child, there is not an ounce of your body that does not feel love.

Love drawn from your body, milked from your pores. You will tell yourself there is not a thing you would not do, no violent death you would not endure for this child. And all that love you feel, all that honest affection, won't protect them from the things you will do to them. From the things they will do to themselves.

Meg stayed with her mom for two months and didn't answer my calls. I cleaned the house and waited. Made it so everything was as it was before we went to the carnival, before the carnival went to us. Then she and Jackson came back, and for a while we didn't talk about it.

***

It took a year for Jackson to feel comfortable with me. For him to trust me to throw him in the air and catch him on the way down.

I had severed a part of his childhood: not a vital part but an important one. That kind of violence, it's a scary part of the world, and it's something he learned from me. And I pay for it. Whenever I see him, I think about what's hiding behind his blank stares, what kind of anger is hidden within my son. Is it real? Did I put it there? Or was it there to begin with? Deep down, inside his soul, is something twitching?

I imagine the phone call, the news that he's strangled his girlfriend in a roadside motel. That he's come into work and shot up the place. That during the last two decades he's been busy hacking drifters into pieces. I don't know if other parents feel this way, if we all chronicle our guilt and wait for the day it comes back to slit our throats. Maybe he's just what he appears to be? A good kid.

LEVI'S SONG

Call me Whale. If there is anyone out there, assume
that you are dead. I have come to a stop; I am stopping. The
cumulative poison is finally at a threshold. I glow from it,
from its strange leaking, virescent blood. Perhaps I'm finished.
Perhaps the world really ends.

I do this to prevent encroaching madness, a craziness that
seems to physically shape itself in the waters around me. I am
going to sing. I am going to project myself through this strange
inky blackness that I dwell in. I shall task this diminishing
ocean with my history, as it tasked me. Let it float through this
wasteland as a final dead record. Listen. The world ended. I
was there. Few are the creatures that remain, if any. I may have
found them all in my wanderings. It seems to have been my
fate to find them. I see ghosts, I keep ghosts in my repository
soul. Even the squids, whom I long assumed did not have souls
as they are dirty, revolting creatures.

It'll sound a little bit human. A little like dead human
Jonathan Pryce. Human talk is a thing that happened to me
when they put all the science inside my brain, and the speaker-
box in my forehead. I'm not sure how much time I have left,
perhaps I have it all, to me death is not an assurance. Listen.

Here we go.

***

It has been countless migrations since I last saw the thing that looks like me. Other examples of what I am. What I am is a whale. I know this because the things that used to murder things like me called us that. Humans. They called us whales. They called us whales and stabbed us with sharp sticks when we tried to breathe. This occurred from the moment these naked apes could paddle into the sea in hollow wood. It increased, exponentially when they got really good at it.

For a brief two hundred years it was a holocaust. We were slaughtered in every way imaginable, hung up on the sides of ships and stripped of flesh, blood and bone. Boiled into jelly and packed into wooden barrels, our corpses, the backbone of an industry that sought, with earnest, to turn us whales into not-whales: lamps, funny smells, cat food, elegant hoop skirts.

By the time I was born, humans had lost some interest in making sure we were all dead, they mostly killed us by running us over with propellers, by making us go crazy with the sounds of their radios and ships, with what I assume was a general sadistic enthusiasm for making strange noises. I was born into this caustic ocean, this wet expanse in revolt against its inhabitants, my kind, victims of an incompatible world dropped into theirs, an eddy and swirl of noises and toxicity. I can only guess that mankind sincerely hated the idea of the ocean, that it upset them to not be solely accounted for in its chemistry, its business of being the ocean. And so they dropped a bunch of garbage in it.

My relationship with humans is somewhat more nuanced than the rest of my kind. If only because I am the lone survivor of maybe everything. I feel responsible for the dead humans in the same way that I feel responsible for a sad looking rock, or a walrus skeleton reaching out towards another walrus skeleton. I was not so much a subject of mankind's violence, but rather its wacky curiosity. During my stay at the Marine Research and Animal Laboratory, Effervescent Gardens, a man named Abraham Caramel inserted science into my brain, a third eye in the middle of my forehead that bridged my two hemispheres allowing them to see color and communicate telepathically. I was not consulted as to whether or not I wanted to see color and communicate telepathically. The procedure went slightly right which is why I have a speaker box in my forehead that translates my thoughts into the dulcet tones of dead human Jonathan Pryce. The procedure went mostly wrong and now I see ghosts, spectral fish and large, hot-blooded oceanic mammals gliding and sounding in my shifting void, all the poor captives who died in the fall of Effervescent Gardens. They are generally unhappy about the way things worked out.

C'est la vie. This is a phrase I like to use. It is a way of expressing some form of dissatisfaction with the world. I learned it from a drowning Frenchman named Pierre. He called it out repeatedly as he drowned, doomed while trying to free me from a fishing net that I was not irreparably tangled in. The sides of the yacht he had been living on proved too tall for him to scramble back up, his life sealed by the timely disappearance of rope ladders from his simian brain in the impulsive second it took him to swing his idiot self overboard. I watched him die. He scraped his fingers to bone on the side of his floating home, a vessel viciously blessed with the name, *Haphazard*. Could I have helped? Absolutely. Did he ask for help? Sure, going as far as to gesticulate a plan for me to launch him skyward with my tail. I launched him in the wrong direction. I may have done this several times. If you're wondering if I have mixed feelings about doing this, maybe. Do I think I gave up some of my moral authority? Maybe. I had not known at this point that his kind were all but wiped out. I only knew my experience, the propellers lodged in brains and tails, and the oceans on fire as the Murderers' water fortresses rusted and leaked black pods; suffocating under water because to breathe was to roast. The painful science mashed into my brain. I knew that his kind had killed my kind. The joke's on me. Since that day I have been the unwilling repository for the soul of Pierre, as I am the unwilling repository for all deceased ocean life. This is how I came to share my brain with a painfully free-spirited Frenchman.

***

I'll start with my family's suicide. It was, perhaps, formative for me. My refusal to be a part of it, my greatest mark of shame. I vacillate on that last point though. My thoughts on suicide are complex.

It was a gradual thing, and it didn't start out as a suicide plan. Like most suicide plans it started out as a rescue plan for my crazy uncle Dullfin, whom I will refer to as Crazy Bastard, which, after a near lifetime of being hacked apart by ship propellers he pretty much was. Crazy Bastard was, for the most part, an abject burden upon our pod, a fifty-year-old bull incapable of taking care of himself or others, spending most of his energy ranting about Whale God and randomly bashing one of us with his cranium, often at the same time. He only ever said one thing, stammering it out with apocalyptic excitement, "There used to be factory ships on the surface of the ocean. They burned day and night with hellfire fueled by the bodies of whales. They burned whales so that they could burn whales, so that they could burn whales, so that they could burn whales." He also maintained a stark refusal to sheathe his penis in any way, opting to drag it behind him in his wake, making everybody a little bit uncomfortable.

One day, Crazy Bastard had a moment of clarity about who

he was and what he was doing. The moment of clarity came when a propeller scooped out one of his eyes and scrambled his brain back into working order. He stopped swimming. He stopped eating. He stopped trying to breathe. He became more articulate. He started saying that the end was coming, that from the butchery of our bodies a whole world had been built, and that world had brought a dirty great tide. A sky of fire, a world of sea. Which sounded pretty okay to us, not knowing the connections between things.

And so, we put him on our backs, bobbed his deflating half-corpse around the coast of Maine and begged him to find silver linings. We should have let him give up. It was his pain. And when he decided to die, we shouldn't have decided to die with him. That's what killed us. Our whaleness. But then again, at that point, I think they were all eager. My family. They had already given up because the world had started becoming strange. Because the things he prophesied were already true. Squid were scarce, taken from our mouths, and hunted by great nets, poison in the water made mother's milk fatal. The currents that told us time and season, lost in an endless barrage of transoceanic activity, the whines of great machines overhead, the invisible tweaking of signals in the air.

One day, when his attendants were busy with the war-on-squid, Crazy Bastard decided to take himself out of the equation. He decided to relocate himself from the coast of Maine to inland Maine, making it as far as a rocky patch called Crescent Beach. Pierre says murderers used to eat figurative crap there and sling each other around at high velocities. He says he once almost bumped uglies on a Ferris wheel. I have told Pierre to stop interrupting. Crescent Beach is my family's graveyard. Crescent Beach is the place where my parents, siblings, cousins, etc. threw themselves after Crazy Bastard in an effort to return him to the water, but really to join him because they were tired and hungry, and the odds of survival didn't look good. It's the place where invisible hands crushed the things inside them that made them work. Where I saw them flop, and wheeze, and slowly stop moving. Where I watched, paralyzed, as my sympathy failed me, my love for them and me and my kind sputtered to a puzzled stop. Pierre says that it's gravity that kills a beached whale. Pierre wants me and you to know that one summer he visited a cousin in Lyons and raced go-karts while high on MDMA.

***

It was because of my family's suicide that I had the misfortune of having science crammed inside my brain. After my refusal to beach, I swam up and down the coast trying to gather the courage to do something self-destructive. In the distance, I saw giant, black birds circling over the lumpy mass of my family's carcasses, hordes of half-naked humans watching in a throng, their flash bulbs capturing the incident in perpetuity. All the while I swam up and down, spouting and crying and willing myself to swim onto the sand and join them. But I didn't, couldn't, a fear to exist propelled me away, while my love for my family kept me in death's orbit. Eventually a boat started to follow me, tracking my every breach as I squealed up and down the shallow coast in a frenzy. I had, as I would later learn through telepathy, become a talking point among the human public, my grief and orphanhood tickling a strange sympathetic streak that compelled them into thinking that my survival was their moral responsibility. They acted on this by shooting me full of a magic liquid that made me exceptionally tired and uncaring. When I could no longer swim, they hauled me out of the water and onto the deck of a small boat, where my own body seemed to crush itself as I skirted around the edges of oblivion.

This is where I first met Pierre. He emerged from the

shadows of the aft, face illuminated by a burning stick that drifted and dissolved into the monochrome twilight of my vision. He was humming softly, his smokey breath spicing the air with a pungent choke of something vegetative and rank. He hugged my flank and said, "Dormir Grand Ami. Tes ennuis disparaissent. Come La pluie dans la grande mer." Than he exhaled a billow of his herbal assortment into my blowhole, and I drifted downwards into a vortex of dark nothingness.

***

When next I woke, I was a prisoner of Effervescent Gardens, a sprawling animal research laboratory built into the rocky side of the Pacific Northwest, designed and run by an eccentric- philanthropist-billionaire named Abraham Caramel, a man obsessed with unnecessary things like animal telepathy. My captivity was a column of water in the center of the facility, extending one thousand feet downward to the craggy ocean seabed, a place forested with barnacled stilts of corroded metal. It was down here that I prepared for my role as last creature, my coming life as ghost keeper. Here I watched, and could see the full, categorized extent of ocean life, sealed in their own compartments by a spiraling corridor of vacuum that corkscrewed around my cell so as to make me visible to the human throngs that paraded through.

In the daylight hours the dry corridors were filled with parades of gawking humans, their doughy young prone to flattening their greasy faces against my tube and smearing themselves. Through my column I could see, but not speak, with my fellow captives: the fleet of Manta Rays in Caribbean Cove, the treadmill idiots of the Salmon Run, the three progressively more insane Whale Sharks that spent their lives in vapid circles. It was here, in the utter shredding silence of my cage that I learned the importance of hearing voices, the underlying hum of the world. In the silence, I had to make my own hum, my own voices, and if I hadn't learned to hear them, I would have lost my sanity completely.

**

Pierre was in charge of feeding me during my time at Effervescent Gardens. Each rising and falling of the sun he would drop clumps of frozen squid into my tank and scuba in with me while I ate, retrieving small bits of squid I had missed in my haste and inserting them between my teeth as I swam to avoid him. When I dived to the depths of my cell he would hitch on to my tail and try to come with me. I think he may have almost died a few times doing this. Sometimes at night he would come and visit me, singing in French under the star smeared heavens, the twinkling ocean above. I would surface and snort at him to stop, the high pitch of his voice like angry lice in my ear. This only seemed to encourage him, to make him think that I was playing the same game. One time, when he wouldn't stop with *La Vie En Rose*, I breached and tried to bite his head off, which he misinterpreted as a gesture of eternal brotherhood, commemorating the moment with a tattoo on his bicep.

Occasionally I would be bribed into some form of human ritual that involved jumping through hoops and splashing with my tail. Pierre would whistle and raise his hand and I would breach or wave a flipper. When I say I was bribed, I mean to say that sustenance was withheld until I gave in and slammed my tail and splashed the villagers, my sole vengeance in this embarrassment being to urinate in the water beforehand.

If there is one positive thing I can say about Pierre, one bare sliver of compliment, it is that if Pierre had been given the choice between being a human and being a whale, he might have made the right choice. At the very least, he was a somewhat neutral soul uninterested in spreading the violence that his kind craved. He was, is, a careless thing whose only interests were, are, pleasure and knowledge. After gaining telepathic access to his mind, I learned all about the miscellany of humankind. As a repository of someone else's information, he has been somewhat useful, as useful as any of the ghosts that have colonized my mind are, drowning my whale-hood with their inner monologues. Perhaps I am no longer my own organism, my own voice, perhaps I am a multitude.

***

When the lights went off and the mostly harmless humans went home, the dangerous ones came out, specters in white coats led by peg-legged Abraham Caramel. He dressed like a lunatic, in a blue captain's jacket with gold cuffs rolled up to the elbows, white breeches that fed his legs into one massive knee-high boot and one gleaming obsidian stump, gaunt eyes like skull hollows, the only feature of his face visible through the shaggy vines of silver hair that strangled his face. He was angry at us ocean denizens, I remember sensing, angry over having lost his leg to a sea urchin's poisonous spine during an unfortunate snorkel excursion, but also angry at the sea in concept, as if it defied him, as if its low potential for his own habitation was a grave miscalculation.

In his nightly walk, Caramel was death itself. The whale devil. He led his pod of surgeons to any exhibit and creature that captured his fancy, and they would nod and slap each other on the back and the next morning the creature would have disappeared. If they did return, they were altered, tails replaced with propellers or supplemented by entirely new outgrowths of flesh: a seal with two heads, a shark with testicles, and a tuna that grew other malformed tuna from its flanks.

I cannot recall when it was that my turn came. I have

always measured time through my movements, the flow of nutrients and current. I do remember that Carmel had started coming to my tank before sunrise, dangling his obsidian peg in the water and proselytizing from a soggy tome of apocrypha, begging me to bite the tasteless appendage off, working himself into a spittle-drenched frenzy that would eventually tire him into unconsciousness, whereupon Pierre would come to drag his prone body away.

The morning he arrived at my tank sober I knew my turn had arrived, afraid and hopeful that whatever he did might lead to an end. What followed was a dream of pain; a sweet fragrance filled my tank and the world receded. Somewhere in the nothingness the Whale God came to me, a giant oceanic current in my shape, slightly darker than the great wash of deep blue that filled my unconscious vision. As my thought expanded this whale shape became filled with the strange connections my mind was making, shapes and sounds and smells, an expansive texture of all things above and below. But there too was something corrosive to this vision, for much of what I saw ran negative, fuzzing and disruptive; the pure thoughts of living things were lost in a buzz of something metallic and larger. A dirty tide.

When existence returned it was in bright new colors, and the shapes behind shapes, and the dreams and memories of all creatures I came into contact with would never leave me again. My brain was heavier, plugged into an invisible sphere of knowledge, my thoughts shaped and reshaped in different ways, leaking Jonathan Pryce words from the speaker box in my head. I felt a new compulsion, a need to see and categorize others, to explain their particulars and functions. Pierre thinks I was to be some sort of an animal tour guide engineered to recite information about each exhibit while continuously emanating Wi-Fi.

***

178

The end of the world was a gradual thing, already in mid progress at the time of my capture. It started in earnest due to the Urchin Fervor, a malignant virus engineered by Abraham Caramel to murder the specific Echinoderm that had robbed him of his ability to water ski. While the urchin remedy had enough success to warrant champagne and an after-hours party, it also had the unintended success of murdering a terminal percentage of most other life forms. The humans who came to gawk at me rapidly decreased in number and those who did were sickly with projectile vomit, often slouching to the floor and crying, eventually curling inwards on themselves and dying as a small bundle of tortured limbs.

I would have starved in this anarchy if it hadn't been for Pierre, who had taken to illicitly living in an aquarium broom-closet after a local baker sought to forcibly wed him to his impregnated daughter. When he wasn't avoiding marauding scientists gone native, Pierre found time to feed me, barely keeping me from starvation. The day came when we ran out of frozen squid, and he made the executive decision to start feeding me from the other exhibits. I've never forgiven this. I'm not sure if it was something I would have done if science hadn't been put inside my brain, if I hadn't been turned into Wi-Fi. But, as it was, with my increased awareness my starvation had been given a new depth, deeper than the melancholy I had experienced when food escaped me, a thought-driven, obsessive hunger. And so I ate them, I ate them all, rotting my soul with each bite of river otter and semi-poisonous starfish. He killed them for me at first, until the specimens got bigger, warm-blooded and doe-eyed. Then he made me do it. With each finished meal I gathered a new ghost, a spectral accompaniment that swam around my vision, a transparent blue wraith. They're reproaching me now. Watching me in this emerald void I have chosen to die in.

This continued for an indeterminate amount of time, enough time for me to become skinny and near to death, until the day Abraham Caramel returned and started shooting the Manta Rays in Caribbean Cove. Ravaged by the violent, early stages of urchin flu, Caramel limped around his mad play-land of nautical puns and fast food, an angry captain of conquest, directing a pillage with verse and a chorus of hot metal, the graceful rays in angelic frenzy, confused by the particles of death eating apart their bodies.

He made his way around the facility and killed what I had not eaten, tapping at my central cylinder and making faces at me, blowing the brains out of manatees and polar bears, requiring an inordinate amount of bullets to do so. I have never seen something more terrifying or comical than that old man and his gun, his mind a shell of vacuous hatred. He wanted to save me for last, my execution a culmination of some narrative fancy that held significance for him. Fortunately, or unfortunately, Abraham Caramel did not live to claim his unreciprocated vengeance. He drowned trying to perforate the Emperor Penguins, the tanks he shot through having flooded the corridor and his obsidian peg leg being a less than ideal flotation device. He died in the used water and urine of those he had dominated, drowned inch by inch in the lunacy of his imagination for other things. I treasure the memory of his final breaths, the slow motion of his frocked corpse floating in the murky green he had unleashed, passing by a quickly submerging civilization of french fry stands and gift shops, stupid banners of nautical puns gently undulating like sea greens, *Effervescent Gardens: Dive into Adventure.*

Pierre released me back into the ocean, into waters that had soured considerably in my time away. The taste hit me like bile. I remember the near silence, the mad drivel of far-off human machines dim and muted in the distance. Pierre followed me into open water in his requisitioned yacht and in a few days, high off watching the mad captain die, I watched him die too.

***

I wandered for an eternity, my sense of time eroded by the unpredictable eruptions and deaths of temperature and current. The coasts were barren, bleached into nothingness by strange blooms of vegetative creatures encouraged into unnatural fecundity by the chemical run-offs that came from the land, swaths of red and green murk that devoured all oxygen in the water, suffocating those that dwelt within. I began to wonder if it was I who caused these events, if they existed before I arrived to see them, or if my seeing them was the cause, because there existed no alternative, just a continual greying world marked only by my own consistent discovery of it.

I searched for my kind, others remotely like myself, large bodies to swim with, friends, mates, enemies. Anything to substitute for, to distract from the babbling swarms of depressed ghosts that swarmed around me, each beholden to its own sad circumstance. I was large at this point, as large as I would ever get, larger than the shriveled ancient I am now. I could swim from the surface to the black depths. If there was something alive, I found it, sounding it out with my mind's voice or seeing it with my new science vision.

Everything I met I ended up betraying, ended up eating, as my awareness of hunger overcame any attachment I could feel: an octopus that collected the skulls of the dead, not unlike myself, except for the constant cackling. A hammerhead shark obsessed with eating the luggage from downed airliners. A group of seals who had learned to raid the flooded coastal habitations of humans, lucking upon a near endless supply of pills that made them see things that weren't there. I wasted my time amongst these lunatics, killing whenever their erratic company proved too annoying, my hunger too great. I murdered the octopus by shouting too loud, I watched the seals waist to chattering husks on their diet of hallucinogenic pills. I saw a walrus eat another walrus. They never left me, these stories, they joined my fleet, my graveyard accompaniment of blue intangibles, schooling around me in a phosphorescent burst of lightning ectoplasm. I sought a place where I could do no harm, a place where none could be done to me. At Pierre's suggestion, I journeyed to where it all began, the flooded remains of Crescent Beach.

And so, I returned to the aquatic tomb of my family, a vast metropolis of strange twisting structures, corrugated loops and spires of metal that hung rusted and monolithic in the green distance, the mottled remains of a boardwalk softened in its eternal soak to a wide brown sponge that lined the distance, pock-marked with the artifacts of human memory: grease food carts, games of simian coordination, a stranded carousel horse that Pierre pretended to ride. He enjoyed himself here, walking up and down this strange wooden purgatory, collecting soggy stuffed animals and wallets, singing La Mer till I tried to make him more dead. And I, at last, found my family, their vast repository of bones littered along a pleasant swath of sand. A ghost city of bleached and pearlescent ribs, and skulls in the sea gloom. I pretended to hear them, and although they could not join my ghosts, I felt as if their voices were real.

I did all that I could to remain at the bottom with my pod, sleeping in rare snatches, gliding upwards as the sounds of life accosted the conscious portion of my brain, waking in the raucous swells of an ocean at war with itself, the night sky hidden by a churning green froth that hummed with angry blades of lightning, swung about by tornados and waves.

One waking, I rose to a flat surface of grey, the water mirror-like, cut by the lip of a roller coaster that curled above the whitecaps, where the blue form of Pierre sat and waited for the sky to reveal a rare calm light. There I had the strangest hallucination. Overhead a streak of fire journeyed across the sky, into the heart of the land that remained, somewhere deep in the place my brain called Maine. When this blaze met the horizon a great column of yellow erupted, bulbous and angry, a great coral of sick cloud that rose up and into the heavy clouds overhead. The entire cosmos was still for this event, this ominous pallid growth that grew and grew till the whole sky took on its dread pale. Pierre's ghost watched ashen faced. Oddly, though our minds are fused, he kept some autonomy over this event. Whatever this destruction was, it meant something to him, as the worst things I have seen have meant something to me. That moment led me here, to my place of death, to this indignant iridescent destination. Later, I heard a voice in the distance, leagues away, a moronic grumbling that repeated when all had gone silent, the sole noise in all my ocean. My ocean. I felt a glimmer of hope that a living world might still be out there for me. And maybe I desired to destroy it.

I could not understand what the voice wanted. It was human, but the repository of language in my brain could not decode it, being only fluent in English, Spanish, and Mandarin. But Pierre understood, told me I would be pleasantly surprised. As it turns out, Pierre had an agenda, or I did, or... It's starting to get confusing. I'm very, very poisoned at the moment. So, let's see, I left my job as grave tender, which I really enjoyed, if you can call watching the bones of your relatives enjoyable. And I sought the source of this noise because it was there, always there, a thing to be uncovered. It was not a good choice.

On my way I had a vision, or I'm having one now...no, it was then. Stay focused. I saw the Whale God, or what remained of it, its living beating animal core suffocated. It was an ancient thing, swimming between the remains of two monolithic radio towers, bottoms lost in the navy depth below. The whale-shaped mass was studded with hilts, iron barbs, and strange

plastic tags that beeped and pulsed with different colored lights.
A drifting, reconfiguring collection of human refuse, trailing
an endless net behind it into the green, murky distance, grafted
lights turning off and on in a nonsensical pitter patter of
disappearing geometries. Whale one moment, garbage cloud
the next. Its eyes were eruptions of television static and when it
opened its strange grill-mouth to speak it did so with the voice
of Crazy Bastard garbled through dial-up and AM radio. This
is what it said, "There used to be factory ships on the surface of
the ocean. They burned day and night with hellfire fueled by
the bodies of whales. They burned whales so that they could
burn whales so that they could burn whales so that they could
burn whales." Then it left and I watched it disappear into
the glaucous haze of dead particles. Maybe I am the Whale
God, perhaps this is what I look like, inside my wreath of
ghosts. Poor dead thing. Poor me, alive. Why must everything
be sinister and unexplainable? Why can't it be hopeful and
unexplainable? I should have gone back. I should have known
that I had really lost it.

***

As I journeyed the signal got louder, more defined, a
graveling repetition of monotone static devoid of emotion. I
was eager, Pierre was eager, we hadn't talked much since the
sky apocalypse, and I did not realize what the water of this
place was doing to me, that I was growing painless green
lesions all over my body. And then I reached the source, the
rickety end of my tale. What I thought was a voice, was a final
gasp. A record of death coming from a grounded metal tube
lost in a glowing kelp forest, leaking green iridescence into the
waters and silt.

Wordlessly, Pierre passed through the hull of the
contraption, and turned the call off, leaving us in eerie semi-

quiet, the metallic skeleton twisting and expanding with every current and change in temperature. A submarine carrying death, that is the concept that whispers into my mind. I should have known. I'm sure Pierre did. I have a vision of him going through a house, putting out the lights and locking all the doors.

Let me tell you something. Pierre didn't drown. I ate Pierre. I did. He helped me escape and I lured him into the water, and I ate him. Not only because I was hungry, but because I was mad and filled with hate and he kept singing things in stupid, stupid French. And now his ghost lives inside my brain and colonizes it with his stupid, stupid thoughts, an un-regurgitated Jonah who has never done me wrong. Perhaps this has been Pierre's quest and not mine. Perhaps there is no difference anymore. I am the Whale God. I am the leviathan and the ark. When a whale dies it sinks to the bottom of the sea, where its flesh and blubber is stripped and shared with all that is living.

And so, I sank to the bottom of the sea.

**

It is shallow here. I lie and watch the dusk through the surface. Pierre is crying between bars of *Non Je Regrette Rien*. I watch the stars through the shimmering film above me, rolling in the near perfect quiet. The stars are making themselves visible for the first time in a while.

Clear-headedness. How did things end up seeming so dire, in such a crisis? Everything simply died and the world responded by becoming something monstrous, a perpetual howl. Irreversible. Done. And here I swim, the chronicler of it, chosen by happenstance. If there is a God other than myself, I wonder if he finds it as confusing as I do, or as simple. My one fear is that when it happens, I'll still be here, part of my

185

own collection, another phantom in the graying depths, and on we'll march us ghosts, and nothing will ever be truly dead at last. Perhaps it will be different, my role as leviathan lifted and all this information, sciences and creatures will return to their proper spheres, I among them.

I see all the souls up there, lodged as twinkles in the firmament's black depths. An ocean above with its own gradients of blue. The science in my brain tells me it's all empty vacuum, but the science is wrong. It's a great expansive sea that edges to eternity. So says I. The bright souls expand in their blackness, as I watch, brighten till they reach me through my emerald surroundings, diffusing into silver anemone blooms, the light refracting through the water, combining into a coral network of white radiance. It is my mind. Every thought I ever had. Every creature I have seen. I live and breathe the destruction of all things.

But the network is growing, ossifying overhead into a hard coral of silver light, a reef of all that I have collected. I would like to be home; I would like to rest in my family's graveyard. Perhaps I have the strength. Perhaps Pierre can lead me on, perhaps we could have been better friends. Here Pierre, let us die on the move. I gather my strength, what hasn't rotted in the submarine's blood. My tale is over, sung as I said it would be. If there is anyone out there, assume that you are alive. I'm headed to a coastal beach in Maine. Come visit me there. Perhaps I will be allowed to sink to the bottom of the ocean, and all that I have acquired will spring anew, my corpse the center of a great shimmering reef. The record of this song will hum in frequency among the waves. The world really does end, but maybe, when we are no longer looking, it begins again.

ABOUT THE AUTHOR

John Waterfall is a writer living in Brooklyn and a graduate of the New School's creative writing MFA program. A proud father. Spends most of his time making sure the dog doesn't chase the cats.

Twitter @JohnCWaterfall.